ALONE WITH THE OWL

ALONE WITH THE OWL

STORIES BY ALAN DAVIS

Minnesota Voices Project Number 97

2000

First Edition

Library of Congress Card Catalog Number: 99-68470

ISBN: 0-89823-203-1

Book design and typesetting by Percolator

New Rivers Press is a nonprofit literary press dedicated to publishing emerging writers.

The publication of *Alone with the Owl* has been made possible by generous grants from the Elmer L. and Eleanor J. Andersen Foundation, the Jerome Foundation, and the Target Foundation on behalf of Dayton's, Mervyn's California, and Target Stores.

This activity is made possible in part by a grant provided by the Minnesota State Arts Board, through an appropriation by the Minnesota State Legislature. In addition, this activity is supported in part by a grant from the National Endowment for the Arts.

Additional support has been provided by the General Mills Foundation, the McKnight Foundation, the Star Tribune Foundation, and the contributing members of New Rivers Press.

NATIONAL
ENDOWMENT
FOR THE
ARTS

MINNESOTA
STATE ARTS BOARD

New Rivers Press
420 North Fifth Street Suite 1180
Minneapolis, MN 55401

www.newriverspress.org

Save us from sickness, accidents and addictions,
and protect us from anxiety and the longing we have
to damage ourselves,
for the body is yours, and delight, and ecstasy.

—BALINESE PRAYER

Others because we did not keep
That deep-sworn vow have been friends of mine;
Yet always when I look death in the face,
When I clamber to the heights of sleep,
Or when I grow excited with wine,
Suddenly I meet your face.

—W. B. YEATS

Some people go to church and speak of God.
Why not dance and become God?

—HAITIAN PROVERB

For my Louisiana family—

Louis, my father, Dorothy, my late mother,
Beth and Patti, Jimmy, Robby, John, and Russ—

and for Bill Truesdale

CONTENTS

TRAVELING BY MOONLIGHT

A group of men tell stories at the kitchen table where Phillips is sitting. It's a strange country, he thinks, listening. He's a man who has seen a good deal of it, despite a bad back that requires him sometimes to use a cane. He's a professional traveler, but tonight he broods too much about his health and his marriage. The table swirls around him with smoke. The stories take forever to tell. That is, they take no time at all, because time has been suspended with bourbon and cigarettes, with tobacco and pots of coffee.

The women, including his wife, are in another part of the house telling their own stories, but in the kitchen he hears about men transformed forever into people with electricity instead of blood in their veins, about journeys taken to the faraway boundary waters, where one country becomes another and fish as mysterious as owls sail above the water. "Some of those fish have wings," a bearded man slurs, a weathercaster drunk on bourbon. "Some fly all night without touching down."

When men circle round a kitchen table with nothing but smoke and liquor and each other for company, their stories either make perfect sense or no sense at all, depending on his mood as he listens. He stares away through a window into the sweltering heat of a summer night. There is a shallow, slow-moving bayou a short distance away. It is not quite visible through the window, but he has stood often on its banks and can almost see the limbs of great oaks draping moss over muddy water, feel the slimy scales of catfish, taste the heavy bayou moisture in the air, hear cattails rustle, bullfrogs croak, crickets rub feelers together. The stories that stay with him, the ones that help, are the ones that swerve away from what actually happened, from the clock ticking above the kitchen table. They are told and retold in various places and in various states of intoxication until the spirit of the bayou inhabits them, until the fish from the boundary waters fly into the room.

Among the women, liquor has also been flowing freely, although two women much older than the others sit chastely on a sofa holding Sunday missals on their laps. Their knuckles are chafed from decades of dishwater, an ocean of dishwater and work so they can be queens for a day, but the work is never done and neither has ever worn a crown. They expected to discuss the Gospels, but instead found themselves telling stories stitched together from the events of ordinary time. The gossip, the anecdotes, the memories fit like a community quilt. Some contribute to it, some wander away; whatever they do, it becomes part of the quilt. There is no right or wrong tonight, but it's getting late and everyone is restless.

Mary Phillips lights a cigarette. "What the hell," she says, and rustles in a storage closet until she locates a bevy of boas, long fluffy scarves of feathers and fur. The younger women put on boas and prance like horses, pawing and snorting, neighing, tasting the air with their tongues. The curves of their bodies, curves men once dreamed about until daybreak, feverish with longing, shimmer like mirages. Mary puts down her glass of wine and opens the shutters.

The women dance in the light of the moon.

Without meaning to, maybe attracted by the pull of the full moon, maybe claustrophobic, they wander out, drape boas over porch swings and white wooden rails, leave them lying like snakeskins in the driveway. Only Mary keeps her boa, wrapping it around her neck and staring into the spray of sprinklers. Lawns all down the block glow mysteriously in a fine spray of water, in the halos of streetlights. "It's my turn to travel," Mary says. Each of the women in turn repeats the sentence. All leave quietly in the cars and cruise under the moon to the bayou where their children sometimes swim. They cross a bridge, leave the road, and come to a stop in a field of grass. They park all in a row, headlights facing the bayou.

The two older women, as if on cue, emerge into the headlights, shielding their eyes from the bright beams as though on stage at some parent-teacher talent show. They have not danced all night, but they dance now, unwieldy, stiff in the joints, short of breath, still holding their missals. "There will be no reading from scripture tonight," Mary shouts from one of the cars. "Heave-ho, heave-ho!" The other women take up the chant and the two older women toss the missals weakly, as if with the last of their willpower, into an eddy of water. "Don't you feel a hundred pounds lighter?" Mary calls out. The younger women cheer and blink their headlights, but the older women stare at the swirling place in the bayou where the missals disappeared.

The men are weary after the stories. Standing up, they stretch and joke about aches. The jokes admit to middle age, a strange new country they have all reached almost without realizing it. Phillips feels his breath catch when the others joke about dissolution, but nobody notices his discomfort. Even if they did, they would try to talk him out of it, tell him to have another drink, because tonight is a night of celebration. Tomorrow, or the day after that, is time enough for consultations with experts, specialists who no doubt have a medication or a treatment that can cheat the grim reaper for years to come.

The weathercaster, wobbly on his feet, returns from the bathroom with an odd, bemused expression on his face. "The women have left," he says. "They've taken the cars." He nods sagely and pulls on his beard. "You know what I think? I think love is political. Yes, political, and more so every year." Phillips laughs politely, clanks his empty glass on the table, but he's unconvinced. Isn't it possible for love to be absolute? The weathercaster gestures broadly as he speaks, as though he's hit upon a new paradigm, then delivers his coup de grâce. "So I say, screw it."

"Yeah, screw it," someone repeats. It becomes the refrain of the evening. The men gather around the weathercaster. After too much to drink, they're all in the same boat. The evening that seemed so perfect to some of them, so mythological, is a little out of whack. The weathercaster, though, is rising to the occasion, adapting his histrionic persona to the mood of the moment and pointing to the door with a grandiose flourish. Everyone goes outside, a little stiff and full of sand after sitting all evening, but ready for trouble; it's as though each man has become self-consciously macho at the same time after an evening in a smoky tavern having a shot and a beer, a shot and a beer, getting drunk enough to go do something crazy. Outside, the weathercaster takes a deep slug from his flask. "Whiskey on beer, never fear," he says, passing it around. In the kitchen, talk was cheap. Out here in the wild night, the moon takes over. Nobody threw dinner plates against the wall in the kitchen. Nobody pulled out a Swiss army knife and scraped initials against the grain into the table. They told stories and good stories they were, too, but out here in the real world talk seems constricting, so they decide on "a hegira, a sacred journey," the weathercaster says. "Something the Indians did, or maybe it was the Muslims, I forget which. Anyway, let's go somewheres."

"Where?" Phillips says. He is holding tight to his cane because his back aches. It's more a walking stick really, crooked and knobby and polished to a high sheen. Tonight is only a brief respite; he must travel again tomorrow. If the stories he hears are good enough, maybe they'll come to mind and keep him entertained when he's on his way to nowhere. He remembers that once upon a time he believed in the power of language and human connection. Tonight, he's frightened. Maybe I don't belong anywhere anymore, he thinks. Maybe that's where I belong.

The men set out for the bayou on foot. "Yes, that's where we'll go," the weathercaster announces. "For one thing, we can walk there. For another, it's a bayou. It's made of water." Several of the men applaud his logic. "Water," he says, then takes a deep, ragged breath and coughs. "Water." He makes eye contact with each man in turn. "It's good stuff."

Phillips pauses and leans on his walking stick to light his pipe.

Pipe in hand, he falls behind the other men but doesn't much care. He is aggravated with them and finds himself longing instead for the company of women, for the stories women tell, for the way they talk. He rubs his unshaven face and remembers without warning how the whiskers on his father's face felt when his father had a face. Nothing but bone and ash now. Remembering his father becomes a passageway to another world. Walking slowly, he breathes in the night air and he travels. One day when he was still young, he touched his father's lips when they were hot with fever. His father was sleeping with the help of tubes and medication, and he kissed him gently on one cheek, kissed him as hurriedly as he kisses his wife when he's on the way to nowhere, kisses her negligently, almost like an afterthought on one cheek, but this kiss he gave his father was no afterthought. It was a kiss he was able to give only because his father was asleep, maybe never to wake again.

Anxious about his health and his marriage, feeling his body speak eloquently about mortality while his soul—or whatever people call it these days—contemplates separation, Phillips has never felt closer to his father. Love does make the world go round, he thinks, though the thought is too embarrassing ever to say aloud. His father never had time for him; he was a workaholic who believed in the bottle and the belt. Gin was his drink of choice. He kept the bottle under the kitchen sink and the belt was always around his waist, holding up his pants, or it was hanging from a nail on the hallway wall where he could get it quick if somebody needed a good beating. He would come home from work, unbutton his shirt, loosen the belt, and scratch luxuriously under the band of his boxer shorts before going for the gin. After a few shots to ease out the day's tensions, he would sometimes slouch into his kitchen chair and withdraw into a sour, bitter mood, his bottle and shot glass, his pack of cigarettes and ashtray making small, odd noises on the zinc tabletop as he obsessively rearranged them. He was uninterested in the demands of family life, the small achievements of his kids or his wife, but sometimes the gin made him friendly and he plied Phillips with stories from before the war, how he traveled by streetcar across the city, too poor even to think about owning a car. His own father, belt in hand, would wait up and strap sense into him if

he came home late or drunk. He would talk to Phillips affection-
ately about the beatings he had once received. It was all nostalgia
and the fog of gin, the pain of the beating glossed over by the pleasure of remembering the past. Kids today don't realize how good
they got it, he would growl, becoming surly again, scratching himself viciously, lighting another smoke, and belting down another
shot of gin. The blue smoke swirled around him as he compared
the golden myth of his life, the one he never lived, to the squalor
of his real life, the one he was stuck with.

Lord knows, Phillips thinks, walking again, I took the buckle
end of Dad's belt often enough. Phillips never intends to remember such beatings with nostalgia, far from it, but there were pleasant times when he sat across from his father at the kitchen table and
listened, traveled into an older man's life.

By the time he reaches the bayou, downstream from the other
men, they are squinting across the shallow, muddy water in the
light of the moon, as if moonstruck and frozen in place. The women
have turned off the headlights. They are moving in moonlight,
doing something that does not make sense. The men are scratching their scalps and armpits, swatting at mosquitoes. The weathercaster is stroking his beard. Are the women dancing? Such an odd
dance, bodies swaying, hands moving fantastically as though paint-
ing sky pictures. They don't seem to be women who belong with
these particular men. They seem rather to belong with the sort of
man who has electricity instead of blood in his veins, who explores
the boundary waters where one country becomes another and mysterious creatures with the bodies of fish and the faces of owls sail
above the lakes.

A bullfrog is belching. Phillips can hear cattails in the wind.
His feet are making an odd, pleasant sound as they crush the tall
grass close to the water. The moist green of his suburban lawn dis-
plays a kind of manicured pride, but here grass is presence and
water laps at his feet as though speaking a language he doesn't
know how to translate. He walks into the mud, into the dark, sour
water lapping at his feet. The mud squishes under his soles and

water laps over his shoes. When it soaks his socks, he decides to wade in deeper instead of stepping back. The sound of the bayou is a language he has never spoken, a language he decides to learn. Using his walking stick for balance, he stares across the bayou at his wife, or at someone like his wife who is not his wife, at least tonight. She is someone else, not the woman he knows, someone else's wife, nobody's wife. Her hair is different, curlier, and darker in moonlight than his wife's hair would ever be. But his wife's hair is dark, isn't it? Couldn't that strange woman, so mysterious in moonglow, be his wife?

He is having trouble with the thought. If he doesn't know his own wife, who does he know? It is long past midnight by now, he knows that much, and so he walks in deeper, takes pleasure in his odd logic and in the way the mud sucks off his shoes. He hasn't walked in squishy mud without his shoes since he was a child. It makes more sense to walk into the bayou than to sit around a table belting down booze, filling the air with gas, or standing in the mosquito-riddled humidity puzzling over the women.

Why not take a walk in the water?

He has been thinking of leaving his wife, of living alone. There is someone else in his life, another woman. Sometimes he thinks this other woman is his wife and he should be faithful to her. It makes him dizzy to think about losing his wife. Until now, she has been the woman that happens to him every day, day after day, the woman he puts up with, the woman to escape from when he travels, but he has always believed, almost religiously, without putting it into words, that his real life is elsewhere, apart from his wife. Could such an unspoken belief have anything to do with his father? He knows the stories his father told, but what about the ones he kept to himself, the ones he may have remembered when he was alone?

The water nearly touches his knees. He smells a fishy odor and the sweet scent of honeysuckle. In the moonlight, he sees narrow snakelike slicks of oil drift past on the surface of the bayou. He feels sluggish, like a man daydreaming after falling in love. Swaying in the mild current, propelled by his needs into doing things he knows he'll come to regret but can't stop doing, he nearly slips and sinks; to compensate, he walks in deeper. It's less scary to keep walking than to turn back. If he waded to shore now, he would feel like a fool. The bayou isn't all that deep yet, but a shell on its bottom cuts through his sock and he cries out. Cries out and keeps going. Even at its deepest, the water won't quite reach his chest, unless he's wrong, unless he's thinking of some other body of water. Even so, it's a bayou and there are plenty of snakes. No sooner does he think the thought than he spies one, so close he could reach out and touch its scales. When he was young and swam in bayous for fun, he told himself that snakes swimming on the surface were not poisonous.

His wife is with another woman. They are moving their arms oddly, delicately, hands gesturing his way, legs describing ragged circles in the moonlight. How do they do that, balance on one leg and move the other? So dramatically, and without falling? In a kind of trance. He yelps in surprise when something under the water bumps into his leg, something dead and heavy. He reaches down, breaking the moonlight, getting a shirtsleeve soaking wet, and comes up with a book. Even soaked, its cover has a pebbly feel to it, like a Gideon's Bible in a hotel room. He stands still to catch his breath and gets dizzy, fighting the current, so he lets himself go downstream, away from the women, women he cannot tell apart from this distance. Perspiring in the heat, his sinuses clogged with humidity as thick as gumbo, he kicks himself to a floating position and drifts with the current.

When he thinks about leaving, floating away on his daydream or his need, he thinks about traveling and returning. That is what he has done for years, but this leaving would be for good. Drifting off with a walking stick in one hand and a soggy book in the other, he feels himself sinking from the weight of his clothes. He lets it happen, he sinks, and then, sputtering out water, he stands loin-deep in the bayou, swaying again. It would be so easy to float on his back in the water as warm as his bath, to go downstream sluggishly, gently, as though drifting off to sleep. He was happy long ago when he lived alone and drifted off to sleep whenever he wanted. Living alone was like traveling on water away from the women, but his happiness was a lonely kind of happiness. In fact, he wasn't happy at all in those days. He was miserable, that's the truth, but it was a kind of misery that made him feel alive.

He kicks off again, on his stomach now, fighting against the weight of his soggy pants, using the book like a flipper, paddling with one hand and pushing off from the bayou's muddy bottom with his walking stick. The men are far behind him now. He has no intention of calling out to them for rescue or support, and it would be just as foolish to call out to the women. As though he has eyes in the back of his head, he's certain the women are dancing ecstatically now, oblivious to any man whatever his intentions might be, but he feels forced against his will to check it out, to use his walking stick like an anchor and turn back and fight the current as the water moves around him. He stares swaying at his wife and the other women.

In the stillness the moon re-forms itself on the bayou's greasy surface. The moon is an image that constantly changes in the current and becomes a mirror. Moon, river, book, he thinks. Suddenly he can feel the booze inside him and he's drowsy enough to sleep. The bayou is like a warm bath.

But after all that, after getting lost in the current of an affair the way he's treading water now, his wife is still his wife. What makes him think giving over his marriage will make him happier? The affair, if he continues with it, will probably follow a familiar course, one known to men and women the world over. First it's wonderful, full of surprises and sensations, like eating a kumquat; then it goes a little bad, full of guilt and anxiety, as though traveling in a plane with one engine kaput and the pilot drunk; and then it's over, or then the marriage is over and the affair becomes something more permanent, something to begin to travel away from. It may not be his wife he wants to leave, he thinks, but something else, something inside that he won't face but won't walk away from, either.

Arrival, departure. Exposure, denial. Invitation, retreat. "Story of my life, man," he says aloud, talking to the bayou, which seems to be listening. He holds to his place far from either shore. Why not let go with the current and see where he ends up? After spending so much of his life on the road, too many nights in too many hotel rooms alone with his traveling samples, it might be fruitful to let go. New wife, new life. But he is also free to engage the bayou, break the moon, part the water with rangy, liquid sweeps of his hands until he reaches the cattails and makes his way, dripping muddy water, to the women. He is free to enter their ragged circle, if they will have him, to open the book and read from it. His wife would be amazed to see him like that, stumbling waterlogged into a New World like a wayfarer or a petitioner. But once he was inside that small circle, once he had shaken off weeds and breathed in something for a while besides bayou reek, would he beckon to or look away from his wife? And what would she do? If he looked away at that crucial moment, the marriage would be history, why pretend otherwise? If he beckoned to her, on the other hand, it might make sense, might feel right, to court her again, to be courtly. If she became his fate, freely chosen, not a bubble waiting to burst, he could learn who she was all over again, and she might be willing to learn the same about him. Unlike his father, someone given to him always and forever and carried like the bedroll of a bindlestiff wherever he goes, someone who taught him that life must always be elsewhere, he can choose to be with his wife. His real life need not be elsewhere anymore. He can look back without turning to salt. He can let go of the past without forgetting it.

It's a nice thought, anyway, to know his father is a man like any other man, not a god whose glare diffuses all pleasure and fills him with a nameless anxiety. Standing in the bayou and swaying the way a child might sit in a tub in very warm water and nod his head to a rhythm nobody else can hear, he tells himself that his father is a man who died, not a face in heaven following him wherever he goes, not a friend, not an enemy, but a man like any other. I loved him, but he wasn't always kind or loving in return. It is a thought he's had before, and each time he repeats it he wants to cry. His father has gone to heaven, or hell, or to his grave. What he is, Phillips thinks, is what I remember.

It's a conversation he's had with himself too many times. Half-floating now, half-gripping the slippery bayou bottom with his toes and walking stick, he stares into the waterlogged moon. He can smell his shirt hanging heavy. It smells like the bayou, and he cringes, standing alone, thinking about those years with his father, his teeth chattering even though the water is very warm. Everything is gone and he has never felt so wretchedly alone, without the stories, the jokes, the flying fish, the land that goes on forever. Without the women.

He tosses away the walking stick but still holds to the book. He's more than halfway across, determined to fight his way back to his wife. His courage and confidence flare up. He's not so old that he can't make his way across a bayou the way he did years ago, but he's not young either. He no longer thinks of himself as brave or as a man of destiny. He has become a man who travels because that is what he does. He's dizzy. Water is no longer the only thing on the move. The bayou, the mossy shadows of the oaks, the ghostly shapes blocking the moon, the moon itself, all seem to be traveling.

Still holding the book, he dogpaddles against the current, which is stronger than he expects but not so strong that he must let go of the book or give up. If he lets go of the book, what can he say to his wife without it? If he holds to it, it will impede his progress and he will come ashore somewhere downstream far from the women. The book has become a problem. He is fighting through the water now, losing his breath. A snake, or something that feels snake slimy, bumps against his leg underwater. Struggling for deep, hoarse gulps of air, he lets go of the book. It swirls away, its cover and soggy pages flapping. With one hand he unbelts his pants and lets them go too, feeling the buckle slide through his fingers, kicking off the pants while treading water, getting a little water in his lungs and choking, floating a little farther downstream.

He begins to swim hard now, fighting upstream back to the women. His shirt, soaking wet, is like a second skin around his torso. He is not very good at swimming, but he is good enough, holding his chin above water, imperceptibly getting closer to shore.

The women are dancing, legs and arms and their own torsos swirling seemingly without effort, so much energy, light, and shadow coming into play.

He must make up a book, a book that does not depend upon the past for sanction, a book his wife will read by moonglow, a book about men and women both, about ordinary time and fantastic things. He thinks about the book as he swims in his unwieldy way, getting a little more water in his lungs, coughing it up, tempted to give up and sink or float away but refusing to give up. He will sink soon enough, float away into the oblivion that awaits everyone. Why hurry the matter? He can feel muddy water like soup inside his boxer shorts. The brown energy of the bayou soaps his entire body. His back aches and begins to cramp up. All evening he listened to men tell stories and to the bayou speak its strange, necessary language. Now he listens to his own body, swimming, listens with the same careful attention he will try to bring to the stories the women tell with their bodies as they dance. Even with his bad back, as painful as the hinges on a door broken by the wind, his body feels stronger than he was brought up to believe it could be. He cringed under his father's gaze and came to mistrust his strength. Now he untangles himself from his shirt, tosses it away, and listens to his body labor. There are clues in his breathing, in the slapping sounds his hands make in the water.

He thinks about swimming, he is all there, putting his energy into the act, but another part of him meditates on the book his wife will read. It will tell his wife things she has never known about him. It will speak to her even when he might prefer to keep his secrets. It will tell stories about the father who sat at the kitchen table grinning into his glass of gin. The things the book tells will be true, even if they never happened. He will be able to say anything, the things he has heard that make sense and the things he was taught but no longer believes.

As he churns his feet, touching bottom and walking again, getting close to shore, thinking that he has a chance to emerge a changed man, eyes cleansed of doubt, as he slaps his hands through the water and makes up the book his wife will read by moonlight, thinking that the mysterious flying fish with the face of an owl belong in the book, that betrayal and trust both belong in the book, that anecdotes and gossip and episodes of ordinary time belong in the book, that penance too belongs in the book, that love belongs in the book as well, that love for his wife might become a part of the book, might become a practice if not a faith, as he thinks all of this, about brushfires overseas, about losing his hair, about people trapped in themselves, the night rises beyond the moon and he is traveling alone again. There is no moon. The night swirls around him like dark granite and he cries out. The women, one of them his wife, help him crawl ashore, without flippers, without clothing, but rising now and standing on his own two feet, gaining purchase on his breathing again. He has gone places for years, made a living going places, but he has never been anywhere, never in his life attended to a place. That has been his place. Now he lets go of that, of nothing, and for the first time, without a passport, he enters a country that is strange, a country he no longer knows, and finally finds his voice and reaches out to take the hand that is offered, a hand that feels very familiar in a darkness with no beginning and no end, and he begins to speak, no longer thinking of himself as a traveler but as someone who will arrive momentarily.

THE SOLID EARTH

I saw many patients before I gave up counseling, but I have never been able to forget Tod Thomas, the first one. Tod was very white, almost clear, the color of bread dough except for tattoos. A blown-open rose graced the back of both of his hands, a purple heart with an arrow through it adorned one of his upper arms, and on his chest the word MOM was spelled out in purple letters two inches tall. He and I had the same build, the same facial features, and in a better world could have been mistaken for brothers. He told me he was in the mental ward, and in prison, because he had lost his insides on an offshore oil platform in the Gulf of Mexico. "I'd sue if I could, Mr. Falcon," he said, playing with the earring in his left ear, "but Mama ain't no rich. No sir, Mama ain't no rich.

"I went deep-sea diving," he told me, "deeper than people go. I'd forget where I was and dream about the fish floating past me. The water was deep, there was hardly any light. All kinds of fish in the salt, strange fish. I was a free man then."

He sat across from me in an olive-green hospital gown at a plain wooden table that teetered. There was a radio on the table and sometimes Tod rotated the dials or ran his fingers along a crack in the plastic cabinet. He would get a dreamy look in his eyes and count under his breath, as though holding to the thread of his story despite a prodigious eruption of unconscious imagery.

In the water, he said, he would study the bowels of the semi-submersible rig, do what he had to do to the drill pipes, daydream about the fish, and return to the platform, but he was down deep so long sometimes that he had to spend an hour or so in a decompression chamber before he could stand unencumbered again in open air. One day, he sat on the toilet in the chamber and something went terribly wrong. A vacuum of air sucked his guts right out of him. They rushed him by helicopter with his entrails in a plastic bag to a hospital, to Charity Hospital as a matter of fact, where they put him back together, more or less.

It is a story that frightened me when I heard it for the first time and one that still frightens me today—a man losing his insides so quickly and never quite getting them back, at least not the way they were.

"That's why they have me here, Mr. Falcon. The company charged me with a crime so I couldn't sue them for the loss of my insides." He reminded me to write it down in the small notebook that lay open before me, though sometimes his eyes went glassy instead and he ran a fingernail from the crack in the radio's plastic cabinet to the underside of one of his arms, where there were many scars, some of them tiny slits, some wide and deep, each a testimony to an act of self-mutilation. "When they stitched back my insides," he said, "some doctor got mixed up and put things in the wrong places." He turned dreamy and started counting again. I wasn't sure whether to write down that part of his story or not, but I knew he would tell me the same story in the same words the next day and the next and the one after that, so I nodded and doodled on the notepad. "Good God, that's awful," I said, because I knew he wanted me to say it and because there was nothing I could do for him except sympathize.

I spent an hour with him almost every day in that bare room. A single bulb in a cage dangled between us. There was a window with metal bars on one wall. Sometimes through it I could see blue sky. Sometimes heavy Gulf Coast clouds scudded past. Next to the window was a nail where I hung an extra pair of pants in case I spilled coffee. (In those days, I was a klutz.) I would look at the pants with their crease still intact and congratulate myself on my foresight, but I lived to regret that spare pair of pants.

"Two hundred and twenty-six," Tod said, and snapped back to

his story. "So you see, Mr. Falcon, I'm supposed to be a free man. Tell them I'll sign a paper. I promise not to sue if they put me on parole. My hearing is next month."

"Great," I said. "I'll see what I can do." I made a note of it.

In those days I had no other life. I was either working or recovering from work. I sat all week in that bare room with only a duty nurse and a dozen inmates for company. I came to know every stitch on my checkered coat, every crack in the wall of the room, every strip of peeling paint.

"Where are my cigarettes, Mr. Falcon?" a prisoner would ask. "I need a smoke." I would shake my head. "This is a hospital. No smoking in the wards." Tunny Dorsey, an Irish American hippie who wore his hair in a ponytail, would enter my office. His every waking moment was devoted to comic books, to villains and superheroes. In fact, he was in the mental ward because he had once confided to a prison psychologist that he dreamed not of people but of comic book figures. "Counselor," he said, "everybody is good or bad. What are you?"

"I give up. What am I, Tunny? A little of both?"

"Don't cop out on me, Counselor." He had a year left for aggravated assault, but somebody outside kept him supplied with comics. It seemed that inside or outside hardly mattered if he had his comics. "It is my salvation, man," he said when I told him my theory. His favorite was the Justice League of America. "Once the Flash vibrated so fast he opened up a passage between Earth 1 and Earth II, where the Justice Society of America was at. You didn't know that?"

"Nope."

"Don't worry about it. A lot of people get them mixed up. The Justice Society and the Justice League, I mean. The distinction is very important, Counselor."

"What do you mean, Tunny?"

"Never mind, I've already said too much. But you know about Superman, right? And you like him?"

"Sure. Who doesn't like Superman?"

"Yeah, right. And Batman, Wonder Woman, right? Man, she fills out a uniform, don't she?" He bit his lower lip and grinned slyly. "But what about the Flash? What about Elongated Man? Aquaman?"

I smiled. Aquaman sounded like Tod in diving gear.

"They had their headquarters in a cave for a long time, then they got themselves a satellite. They had matter transporters in every town so they could reach a crisis in no time flat." He snapped his fingers.

"Matter transporters. Like on *Star Trek?*"

"Better, dude."

"Makes life here seem awful dull, don't it?" I said, squinting because there was a bright rectangle of glare on my desk.

"But there was a war between Earth and Mars, and the president banned all metahuman activity."

"Metahuman activity?" I liked how it sounded. "What are you, Tunny? Villain or hero?"

"Me? I'm Snapper Carr. He hung out with the superdudes. Sometimes they made fun of him, teased him, you know what I'm saying? They didn't tend to his needs, but your job is to take care of me. Right?"

"I'm your counselor, Tunny, if that's what you mean."

When he left, a gaunt man with dark bruises under his eyes who had served as a medic in the war took his place. His name was Prescott. He was grinning. "Counselor, what you study in school?"

"The novel," I said. "I've already told you that." He was having himself a bit of fun, I could see.

"Say what?"

"You know, fiction. I tried to decide if the novel was alive or dead."

"The novel." He turned away from me and let fly a gob of spit. "People make that stuff up, don't they?"

"That's it."

"So what did you decide?" He licked his lips and ran the tip of his tongue over his teeth. "Is it alive or dead?"

I shrugged. "I decided I was asking the wrong question."

- - - - -

I wore my shiny checkered sports coat from the Goodwill store, pinned my identity card to it, and tried to comb my hair each morning so that the nursing staff might mistake me for a professional. I pored over my *Handbook of Projective Techniques* and administered Rorschachs and MMPIs according to a protocol that I pieced together like a detective, hoping to piece myself together in the process, but when I ushered Tod or one of the others from my office and sat down to make sense of what they told me, I didn't know exactly what a case history was supposed to be. Was it my version of their reality, like a writer writing a story? If so, should I include sensory information, the way Tod played with his scars, the way he sucked on his index finger because he couldn't have his cigarettes? Might I predict from his past behavior when another act of self-mutilation would happen? Or should I limit myself to a factual summary of his psychiatric history and past treatment? Tod's story was clearly not true, but it was a good story that explained who he was in a way that I could not. I didn't want to turn it from a story into a "story," but neither did I want to lose my job, so I wrote his case history, piecing it together from the jargon I found in psychology and social work textbooks. Tod had his own life and his own plot, though, and my case history, referring as it did to "affectlessness" and "concrete thinking," to "presenting symptoms" and "milieu therapy," was a betrayal.

On the other hand, he was serving a sentence for rape, so why shouldn't a story of pathology be imposed upon his life? My "story" may have reduced the truth of his life to some therapeutic model that my unpracticed mind did not believe was inevitable, but the story of my own life was disordered, hardly a model of its kind, so who was I to judge? Somehow order had to be imposed on events, and a psychological diagnosis, as inexpert as it was in my hands, made as much sense as anything else did. Maybe there was some principle of justice at work that I wasn't yet able to fathom but would come to understand. Maybe I was stranded on the wrong earth and needed to vibrate as fast as the Flash to find a passageway to a different world, one where Aquaman or Elongated Man could make things right. Still, my case history felt like an act of creative writing. On paper though, once I typed it, it looked like an act of God, like a story contrived to do battle against all the other stories that might be told.

- - - - -

One Monday morning, I had just taken off my checkered coat with its identity card and slung it over the back of my chair when Nurse Florence, who had worked the night shift, accosted me. She closed the door to my office. "I found Tod having sex with another patient," she said. "They was busy at it half the night I expect before I caught on. Lord knows what they was thinking of."

"I can guess," I said.

Her eyes were bright. I couldn't tell if she was outraged at the breach of decorum or a little excited. "You know that little light in the bathroom?" I nodded; it was a bare bulb protected by a wire cage, like the one in my office. "Tod, he had himself a straight pin, and he figured out some way to pinprick that light so it burnt out. He figured to break the bulb piece by piece and eat the pieces."

"Yummy."

Nurse Florence, or Nurse F., was a Creole woman in her forties with skin the color of café au lait and sumptuous breasts that the buttons of her uniform barely seemed able to contain. She was everyone's erotic mother confessor. The prisoners, delighted to be in New Orleans away from the state penitentiary but aggravated by the close quarters, would drag themselves in long hospital gowns from the television set to a table of tattered magazines to Nurse F.'s station. "Nurse F., when we all getting some cigarettes?" "Nurse F., tell Mr. Falcon he got to let me make my phone call." Nurse F. would put her hands on her hips and puff out her chest until I expected every button on her blouse to burst in a display of glory the likes of which none of us would ever see again. But the buttons always just held and Nurse F. would survey her tiny kingdom of sorry-looking men with their asses hanging out of their gowns and shake her head long and hard. "You all in a hospital. This not a picnic park. You here to get treated. You all are patients, but also convicts. You sick people." She would banter with them one by one, get their spirits up, and pass out a few chocolate bars while I adjusted my tie.

"Some diet," I said that Monday, still adjusting the tie. I could never get the knot just right. "Are you guessing or did he tell you all this?" I knew from his charts that his self-abuse included swallowing razor blades, bits of coat hangers, and any other goodies that came his way.

"He told me. Those boys don't keep nothing from me once I get them alone." I didn't doubt her word; she had on a subtle perfume that mixed sensuously with her soapy body aroma and the starchy smell of her uniform. My office usually smelled of flop sweat; her presence was overwhelming. "In fact, I think the boy had a psychotic break," she said. "He fell right into my arms and rested his head against my chest and told me everything."

"He did, did he?" I said. It was exactly what I wanted to do. "What did he say?"

"That he was on the basin with his back to the door so he could reach that bulb. He got taken from the back and pulled down and while they had their sex he ate that pin. To 'enhance the experience,' he told me. He's down in ER. They doing X rays."

"Who pulled him down from the basin?"

"I'll get to that, sugar. Hold your horses." She stepped away from me and moved to the other side of my desk, to the same chair where Tod sat each day. Her body heat was like a third person in the room. "We buddies, ain't we?" she said softly.

"Buddies," I said.

"We look out for each other, don't we?"

"Always," I said.

"What I'm getting at," she said, "I ain't too happy about this incident. I prefer not to report it, is what I'm saying. They let me work these double shifts and I am grateful, you understand, but the truth is, I was snoozing some last night. Look up at me, sweetie." Her eyes, when I finally stared into them, made me dizzy; they were flecked with gray. "You understand me? I'll talk Prescott down. He's the one who was with Tod. He's all upset."

"Upset?"

"Yeah. He feels like he's gonna get the blame for a mutual act. He say Tod egged him on, swished his butt like so until he had no choice but to take some action." I furrowed my brows; it was hard to imagine Tod, with his scars and tattoos and earring, with his little round tummy after too much prison food, with the burst-open roses on the back of his hands and the tribute to Mom on his chest, as the object of anyone's affection.

"Yeah, I know," Nurse F. said, though she didn't tell me what she knew. "Go take an early break," she said, "then check on Tod in the ER. Do you more good anyway if you let me take care of things. Go on now."

I tried to protest, but it was no use. "Great," I said. "Okay," I said, working my jaw muscles, and walked away from her. Prescott, his eyes set off-kilter in a frontal facial plane like an owl, crossed his arms and fixed me with his thousand-yard stare. At a nearby snack bar, I ate a greasy burger. Then, my heart on fire, I went to the corner library and picked out a magazine from the rack. I leafed through it but it didn't seem to be about anything. There were pictures and words. In one snapshot, a celebrity with a deep tan cut a slice of cake; in the next, the same celebrity fed a slice of the same cake to a woman in a strapless gown who also had a tan.

Outside, the city smelled of the Gulf, promised a shakeout, a rip-roaring storm. It was what I needed and what I wanted. The city itself was mostly below sea level, built on a spit of swampy land between the Mississippi to the south and Lake Pontchartrain to the north. It was protected by dikes and levees and drained of underground moisture by pumping stations that worked around the clock. Machines I couldn't even see made it possible for me to stand on the solid earth. On such a day, with the air full of ocean and the ground beneath my feet seeming to float, it was easy to imagine Tod as a comic book character in his diving gear under the city, slashing his way through muck and mud with a prison latchkey between his teeth, his entrails wrapped like a snake around his neck.

But there was nothing funny about the story Nurse F. had told me, and I hurried back to the hospital, ashamed that I had allowed her to talk me into leaving, determined to find Tod. As I reached the hospital complex, I thought of a question to ask him, a question that I imagined would cure him. In a momentary fit of hubris, I was delighted with myself; it was the first time that I had put aside my flop sweat and understood the nature of therapy. Ask questions, I told myself. Ask the right questions. Get Tod to tell the truth. Ask him what he sees, hears, smells, what he thinks, not only what happens but also what he feels about it. To get at the truth, I knew that I needed to know a thing that only Tod could tell me: What does it taste like to eat a lightbulb?

- - - - -

The hospital, always under renovation, seemed to be held up by rusty scaffolding and big rubber bands. It was part of an aging complex that included two medical schools, a museum of pathology that contained mounted specimens of every lesion known to man, and a museum of tropical medicine where a doctor or medical student might examine photographs of the human body as it deteriorated from malaria, yellow fever, leprosy, and the plague. The place had been built before the Civil War, but new wings were added each generation in every conceivable architectural style. The result, a work still in progress, comprised a catechism of endless passageways that I had tried to memorize without much success.

Elevators were numbered randomly (or not at all) and corridors that seemed promising would dead-end or lead me without warning into an operating chamber or a recovery room or the morgue. Each morning when I arrived, I imagined a drawbridge with a moat. Each morning I touched my identity badge as though it guaranteed me safe passage to my new job. Bursting to cure Tod, feeling for the first time like a mental health professional, despite my shiny slacks, my uncombed hair, and my degree in English, I bounded up the steps of the hospital without regard for the large drops of rain that plopped on the sidewalk like eggs frying. For luck, I reached for the badge on my chest, a compulsive mannerism that I repeated maybe a dozen times each day, and then I remembered that it was pinned to my checkered sports coat draped over my chair like the part of me that stays deaf and dumb.

I entered the main building, somehow took a wrong turn, and wandered the corridors the way a lost soul probably travels aimlessly in the underworld. I found an elevator and punched the button and waited patiently for it to groan open, but nothing happened. Two interns in hospital scrubs saw me standing at the elevator door and waited with me until all three of us lost patience and searched together for an alternative. "Fucking goddamn place," one of the interns said. With an elbow, he punched a hole in a newly constructed partition and smiled at nothing, as though the burst of violence was his bowl of cereal for the day. His sallow-faced companion and I exchanged glances. "At least he used his elbow," his companion said, enunciating every syllable as though teaching grammar to a child. "That way, he won't damage his fine surgeon's fingers."

I left them to their own devices, found a stairwell, and took it upstairs to the third floor, but the corridor did not lead to the secured wing. I found myself staring into an operating theater through a glass partition with a group of medical students. There was a moustache of perspiration on the upper lip of the student to my right; he licked his lips repeatedly and made a sound as though he was chewing on saliva. The surgeon below us was slicing open a patient with what I thought was far too little regard for her welfare. Then I realized that she was a corpse and that I was witnessing an autopsy or dissection. The surgeon sliced off little pieces of her and held them up for the benefit of the students, then placed each piece on a tray beside the corpse as though preparing a plate of prosciutto. He lectured on the disease that apparently had taken her life and then beckoned to the students. One opened a door and they all maneuvered single file into the theater. The student with the moustache of perspiration made room for me, but I ignored him and descended the stairwell and wandered the corridors until I found myself again facing the elevator door that wouldn't open.

I turned from the elevator to consider a long dark hallway and saw myself, a figure in a checkered coat staring at me from a shadowy place at a vanishing point below me, as though the hallway tilted and descended. I could only see myself above the waist, but I could not believe anyone else within a thousand miles would wear the same ridiculous coat. "What the hell," I said. I took off my glasses, rubbed my eyes, replaced my glasses and stared again, but still saw a precise counterpart of myself. It was swaying as though drugged. I was stunned. I doubted my own identity. I leaned to the right and imagined the figure in the shadow did the same thing. I'm not myself, I thought, I'm somebody else.

"What are you looking for?" a man's voice said. "Can I help?" I turned, dazed, biting my lower lip. An orderly was smiling faintly at me. "Um, the Emergency Room," I said, remembering where Tod was. He gave me directions. I felt like I was waking after a long sleep, and still dreaming.

In Emergency, they practiced triage at night, when the casualties of the drug wars and the turf wars and of numerous domestic battles were dumped (sometimes literally) on their doorstep, but by midmorning the waiting room was crowded with the merely sick and the merely wounded. Without my badge, I had to argue with the freckled nurse in charge, but finally she brushed a curly strand of red hair away from one eye and told me that a deputy had returned Tod to the mental ward. "I'll call up there for you," she said. The room where we stood was divided with curtains and hospital linen into a dozen cubicles. A resident nearby scrubbing his hands overheard us. "You in charge of that asshole?" he said in a Southern drawl. "I told him I hoped to hell that lightbulb might tear up his insides real good. Sonofabitch passed it without a scratch. Last time you-all brought him down here, he'd had himself a straight pin for a snack. We have enough goddamn trauma in here without baby-sitting some freak. Last night I had me a twelve-year-old girl with a lung pierced by a screwdriver cause her daddy decided she didn't know how to mind. Next time your nut case eats his lightbulb or swallows his straight pin, I hope he tears himself a new asshole."

I sidled up to him. "You doctors are surly today," I said.

He gave me a cross-eyed stare and I laughed. "Work yourself two shifts in a place like this and tell me how much empathy you got for some guy who likes to snack on glass and metal objects."

I wanted to know what Tod looked like on the inside, whether there might be any truth to his story, but the doctor was called away.

"You're to report immediately to the locked ward," the nurse said. "There's been an escape."

"How do I get there?" I said. "I'm lost."

- - - - -

Two security guards had commandeered Nurse F.'s station. I saw one on the phone beyond the glass partition; the other was interrogating the patients one by one. Nurse F., straining to be jovial, stood with the inmates in the open ward. Her voice was too loud. I motioned her into my office, closed the door, and turned on the tinny radio. I sat in my chair and placed my hands on the desk and stared into her gray eyes because one of my books told me that such calm was profitable when dealing with a hysterical patient. She rested her bottom on my desk and crossed her legs. They were very good legs and I wanted to say something to her in the spirit of the moment. I wanted her to cross them someplace else so that I might keep my attention where it belonged, but I didn't know how to broach the subject. "I'm seriously disturbed," I said, truthfully enough.

"I gave Prescott the jou-jou and made him understand where he stood. He said he had a jones for Tod—that's a major crush, you understand—and told me Tod was now his boy-gal. I told him otherwise. Then Tod came back from ER and went looking for you. I took Prescott back to my station to give him some candy.

"Don't frown at me," she said, and pursed her lips. "I bribe them boys with a little candy all the day through, and nothing wrong with the practice, neither. We all like a little sugar now and then." I tried not to look at her legs. "Anyway," she said, "that's when Tod put on your coat with that badge." A muscle in her jaw tightened. "He lucked out, the shifts were changing when he made his move."

"Sounds too easy," I said. "Maybe Dorsey gave him a matter transporter."

"Say what?"

"Nothing." Over the music—disco—I heard voices outside the door. Rain drummed against the window.

"It wasn't but a minute or so before I saw what happened and told the guards," she said. "That boy can't be far away."

"I saw him," I said.

"Say what?"

"I didn't know it was him, but I recognized my jacket." I told her the story and tried to picture Tod staring at me from the shadows near the elevator. What would he do? "If you were Tod," I said, "what would you do?"

"If I was that boy," she said, "I would jump in the lake."

"Go down, you mean?" I puzzled over her remark as though it was meant seriously. The last thing I had expected on my watch was somebody escaping. It was exhausting enough just fending off everyone's demands, listening again to Tod retell the one story he knew by heart, and bearing up as Dorsey quizzed me to make certain I understood the difference between the Justice League and the Justice Society. "I'm a counselor. I should try to find him."

"You leave it alone," she said. "You a free man."

"What's the date today?" I said. "Earth I or Earth II?"

"Stop trying to be cute," she said. "We have our story straight? We on the same page?"

"Beam me up," I said.

- - - - -

Despite her advice, I went looking for Tod. I tried retracing my steps, but it was impossible. I was angry and upset. The labyrinth of corridors and elevators and stairwells swallowed me whole like a boa constrictor and squeezed me until I found myself gasping for air in my frustration, irresistibly counting my pulse. Tod was wearing my pants, my coat. He had my badge on his chest.

I returned to the mental ward and spoke to Dorsey in an isolated section of hallway near the door; someone from security was sitting in my office. "Did he say anything to you?"

"Me, Counselor?" Dorsey said, pulling back his shoulders and tossing his hair so that his ponytail flipped over one shoulder. "Maybe he did like the Flash—*whoosh!*"

Tasting a surfeit of saliva, I spat on the floor like a seasoned convict and motioned to Prescott. "What about you?"

"Who?" Close enough to eavesdrop, he fixed me with a gaunt stare. "You one of the peons now, Counselor. Got to stand in the hallway like the rest of us, I see."

"You know anything about Tod?"

"*Whoo, whoo, whoo.*" He smirked, then the lines around his eyes came tight. "You putting me in the cross?"

"This is between you and me."

"What?" he said. "You a spy? You don't work for Corrections? You don't take notes on your little pad?"

"Listen," I said, "I want to find Tod. That guy's in no shape to be loose." Over his shoulder, I saw a security officer stare our way from behind the glass partition of the nurse's station, but Nurse F., standing beside him, put a hand on one of his beefy forearms and he turned toward her.

"What you know about loose, Counselor? You walk out of here a goddamn free man every day." He curled his lip, folded his arms, leaned back on his heels, and offered me his blank thousand-yard stare. "Look, Counselor," he said, his voice normal in volume but his tone dismissive, "you an expert in dead books. Ain't that right? Who you to judge me? Why don't you go hang in the library like a good student and read one of them dead books?"

- - - - -

I reentered the labyrinth. For some reason, my sense of smell was working like a rock drill. I could distinguish strata of odors as though I was a paleontologist and the air was filled with fossils. I decided to follow my nose. Mildew and mold, the bedraggled sick smells of a large waiting room, the sour odor of urine like vinegar, newly applied mustard-yellow paint and the chalky odor of plaster, vomit and shit overlaid with disinfectant, a smell like soggy newspaper outside one of the cancer wards, the odor of meat loaf and greasy fries when I passed a cafeteria, the smell of hydrogen peroxide and mercurochrome in the hallway outside a small room for patients with gaping holes in their bodies, the flavor of whiskey on the breath of a blue-smocked worker inspecting a wall, the starched stuffiness of a prim nurse on an open lift meant for freight, and many other odors both bitter and mild for which I have no name. My nose became itchier, and finally, after descending a rusty spiral stairwell, I reached a poisonous atmosphere that smelled like the swamps under the city. I sensed that I was far beneath the hospital, deeper into the earth than I thought was possible in New Orleans. The steady rhythm of pumps echoed among huge misshapen pieces of machinery, some pieces alive, quivering and chugging with effort as though on their last legs, other pieces cold to the touch, sweating with moisture and leaving on my fingers streaks of rust like blood.

I found him underneath a piece of such machinery, some sort of boiler unit with thick squat legs and a curved underbelly that left him room enough to curl around it for heat. He was sucking on a jagged fragment of glass tubing and coughing up blood.

I went to him. "Tod. It's me, Sam Falcon." Close-up, I could see that with one hand he was clenching a thick pipe underneath the boiler that ran from its underbelly into the concrete floor where his blood had mixed with swamp sweat to form a shallow pool of liquid the color of cayenne pepper. He was mumbling something as he chewed on the glass tube, but I couldn't hear for the mad din of machines. For a moment I was afraid to reach down and touch him. I feared I might receive an electrical shock or that the pool of liquid around him might be somehow toxic. Then I reached for him and forgot about myself.

I pried his hand as gently as I could from the pipe and pulled him, still in a fetal position, away from the boiler to an open place between machines. His eyes were glassy, his face pale, forehead feverish. He was in such bad shape that I didn't know what to do, whether to hoist him to his feet and to the Emergency Room or to leave him alone until I could find help. He was still wearing my clothes. I buttoned up the filthy checkered coat to give him as much warmth as possible. SAM FALCON, COUNSELOR the badge pinned over his heart said.

He continued to mumble. "What's that, Tod?" I leaned close. Blood was trickling from his mouth and I wiped it with my shirt-tail. It took all of my discipline to lie on the floor behind him, drape an arm over his torso and tenderly massage his bloated belly.

"Sixty-four thousand, five hundred and fifty," he said.

Massaging his belly, I lay with him for a minute or so. "Sixty-four thousand, five hundred and eighty," he mumbled.

I struggled to my feet. "Tod, hold on, buddy," I said. "I'm going for help."

He kept counting. I thought that I would find my way as if by osmosis to the Emergency Room, that the twists and turns of the hospital corridors would shake me out as though from the wrong end of a telescope. It could be that Tod's trance was contagious. In any event, I don't know how long it took me to find a passage to the main hallway, but I happened upon an office with a telephone and called Emergency. By the time I found my way back to the ma-chines, Tod had been stripped of my jacket and badge and placed under blankets on a stretcher. His eyes were closed and he was hooked up to a bottle of clear solution, but he was still counting, the movement of his lips detectable only because I knew what to look for. Two security officers followed the stretcher. They were solicitous of the medical technicians, and of Tod, until we reached Emergency, when one of them, the man with the burly forearms who had stared so hard at me on the mental ward, took me aside for questioning. His questions were senseless and incriminating, and he repeated each one until I wanted to slap him upside the head just for the relief of it, but finally, after berating me to his heart's content, he returned my badge. "You keep this on your person now whenever you're in this building. Is that understood?"

"Roger that, Captain," I said, unable to hide a smirk, and went looking for Tod in Emergency. It was an hour before I found him or, to be more precise, an hour before the surgeon, the same one I had met earlier, found me waiting in an uncomfortable chair surrounded by the sick and wounded. The surgeon was no longer surly but grim. He took me to a small room furnished with a plain blond desk, several more uncomfortable chairs, and a small shrine in one corner to Mother Mary, cast in plaster of Paris and painted in pastel colors. A narrow rivulet of tears scarred both of her cheeks. Above her, catty-cornered, a gaunt Christ dangled from the cross, his eyes looking down on me with pity.

I sat in one of the chairs and the surgeon stood above me. "I'm sorry," he said. "He didn't make it. He was your charge?"

"Something like that." Even after seeing all the blood he had lost, I was stunned. I felt that Tod and I, in our separate ways, had both been trapped in the same mad dream. I had been so certain that I might help him, even effect a cure, by asking the right questions. Now he would never be able to tell me what it felt like, how it helped, to eat a lightbulb.

"That's tough luck. If I were you, I'd take a big breath and let it go." He squeezed one of my shoulders, then gave an accounting. During surgery, they had found nails, tacks, and even a rusty bit from a drill, but mostly several scoops of chewed glass. "Apparently he found a box of tubes and stuff and decided to conduct himself a little experiment, have a little Christmas feast. He was one poor sick fuck, wasn't he?"

He said the words without rancor and I nodded. "Was he conscious at all? Any last words?"

"He didn't come out of the anesthetic, if that's what you mean, but he was counting until we put him under. I wanted to ask you about that. 'Sixty-four thousand, nine hundred twenty-eight,' he said. Know anything about that?"

"I heard him counting. God knows what it means."

"Look," the surgeon said, "I'm going to leave you here. Take a few minutes. If you have any more questions, give me a yell. It's easy to find me, I'm the one with blood on his hands." He sounded bitter and I wondered how many times each week he had to visit this room.

Mother Mary appeared to be cross-eyed. I sat for a few minutes and stared at the soothing pastel colors of her vacant face and her robe as though doing penance after emerging, as a teenager, free of sin from the confessional. Dear Father, I wanted to say, it has been forever since my last confession. Father, I wanted to save him. I couldn't. Please save us all from sickness, please forgive our trespasses.

I thought of my own father, my real flesh-and-blood father, who lived a hundred miles away in Lafayette, and decided to visit him. He was a devout Catholic and would want me to attend Mass with him. I had once been a Catholic myself, more guilty than devout. I ran endless laps around my back yard whatever the weather to pay for my sins and to work off the time that by my own calculus I would otherwise have to spend in Purgatory. Twenty laps for fighting with my father, the same when I jerked off. I owed the Church thousands of laps.

But now Mother Mary in her pastel blue robe and the Christ with his downcast eyes seemed quaint. I no longer knew what to believe. What do we live for? *Nada, nada.* My favorite professor had taught me that the universe was expanding and in many trillions of years it would die. First, in a few million years, the bright stars would go, like the one that gave Earth its life, then other stars and heavenly bodies would ping out one by one, and next, long after sentient life had disappeared from the universe, black holes would gobble up everything else, and finally the black holes themselves would dissipate. Nothing would remain in the heavens but protons, electrons, and silence. "Bodies are either in motion or at rest," my professor had lectured. "All of you sit here calmly for the moment as your thoughts ping out one by one. Consciousness gobbles up everything. The universe gobbles up consciousness. Death awaits us all. I'm surprised you're able to keep yourselves together even for the short time it takes me to say these words."

The patients already knew about Tod's fate and were depressed, more because he didn't escape to the free world than because he committed a kind of suicide. Nobody had much to say to me except for Dorsey, who wanted to talk about the remains. "Are they going to burn him?"

"I don't know. That's for his family to decide."

"If he has any family, you mean. He never talked about nobody."

"Yes, that's what I mean."

"I think I'll get burned when I die. I don't mean no electric chair, I mean ashes to ashes, dust to dust. They can burn me and then throw me in the lake, because I love to swim."

I must have frowned, because he made a hangdog face. "I apologize, Mr. Falcon," he said. "I don't mean to get selfish right after T-man kicks the bucket. But you know what I'm thinking?"

"What's that?"

"It's better to be Snapper Carr than the Flash."

Before I left the hospital complex, I collected my checkered coat. I also thanked the surgeon, who was so busy that he barely seemed to recall who I was. The coat was tattooed with blood. It was not worth cleaning; besides, it belonged now to Tod as much as it did to me. Standing over a trash bin with it, I accepted with a clutch in my guts that Tod was dead, not because I failed to ask him the right questions, but because his insides were gone. When I closed my eyes as if to say a prayer after depositing the coat in the garbage can, I could see him in his diving gear, the oil rig above him in the salt, deeper than people usually go, so deep he forgets where he is and stares hypnotized at the fish floating past him. The water is so deep, there is hardly any light, but he has a lantern with him, a diver's lamp, and can shine it wherever he wants. The world becomes his oyster. Those are the days, the ones in memory that never fade from sight until the very end. The fish down there with him are strange. Even in the dimness of the deep they glow, some silver, others transcendent like the colors of the rainbow, a few golden in the light of his lamp, shedding phosphorescence as they swim. He is a free man down there, an Aquaman. He has his insides.

THE GIVING

All of her stuff had disappeared from her house a piece at a time. Now it was empty save for her bed, a table or two, and the bicycle that she, Patricia, would soon give away. A small Asian bell had gone first and the giving had felt good. The bell of blackened brass had a greasy, much-handled solidity that made her feel intensely connected to a village reality about which she knew nothing.

All the liquor in her cocktail cabinet, along with the cabinet itself and a mahogany buffet on which the bell had been displayed, went next. That second act of giving had felt even better, because the buffet had been a gift from her ex-husband, and the cabinet, as well as some of the rare liqueurs inside it, had been heirlooms. Such a sacrifice was more than merely material. If she did not feel exactly elevated by the giving, it still somehow worked on her lapsed Christian soul like an infusion of grace. In her bedroom, she slipped out of her dress and heels into a striped shirt. There were three messages on her machine.

"Thanks for the sculpture," one said. "It's lovely. It looks a lot like the one in your bedroom. I'm so surprised you thought of me." It was her mother. "You're never home when I call. I'll try again soon."

"The jacket's beautiful," one said. "I've always wanted a black leather jacket." It was Nancy, her best friend, whose voice was low and hard to hear, as though she was speaking, embarrassed, into a cup of coffee. "But I can't take it. You've given me so many things already. That's not necessary. In fact, it feels wrong. It feels a little grandiose. Just let me pick up the tab sometimes, okay? That would be a real gift."

"Can I come over?" one said. "I don't mean right now. I mean when I get off. You know what time I get off. Can I come over? I want to come over." It was Dave. He was the evening manager at the debt-collection agency she managed during the day. "I'm at the office. You know that. I'll call back in fifteen minutes, maybe half an hour. Whenever I finish with the deadbeats. I want you to be home when I call. I want you to feel my vibrations when you listen to this message. This message is a massage. I want you to call me when you hear my voice and tell me to come over. Can you do that? Can I come over? If I come over, you'll feel me coming, every step of the way. Patty?"

As she listened to his voice, a voice so insistent she more or less gave him his way most of the time, she stared embarrassed at the bicycle, hanging from a burnished pewter bracket across from her bed. The bike was a clean white object with black handgrips and a seat the color of bone. It had hung uselessly on the wall since the day she had biked on impulse to a wine tasting and spent the afternoon sampling 102 Chardonnays. She still couldn't remember biking home after dark or placing the bike on its bracket before falling fully clothed into bed, but there it was.

She walked over to it, took it down, and carried it to the front room. Moving with the bike was like working out with weights at the club, like dancing to dizzy music to make her fast-beating heart beat even faster. It made more sense on the wall, where she could stare at it when she felt depressed. She lowered it to the floor, her knees bending and the muscles in her legs tightening. She balanced it on its kickstand like a work of art and leaned back, studying it with hands on hips, the black-and-white stripes of her shirt hanging down to the middle of her thighs. On a coffee table, a beautiful piece of furniture she could not yet bear to give away, there was a magazine, the alumni publication of the religious college she had once attended. On its cover, Christ was standing in a desert with a great, horned owl on one robed shoulder and a baby cradled in one arm. She stared at the picture, frowning, working deep, vertical lines into her forehead, and then stared at the bike, its seat contoured like a cow's skull, as though the two objects were speaking to her about important, unknown things.

As she drew her bath, she thought about how beautiful the bicycle was. It belonged on the wall, where it could be quite useless, a thing to look at and think about. It was not time to give it away, but she had found out that Kate's bike had been stolen, and Kate needed a bike because for Kate a bike was a thing that took her to and from work. Still, what did she owe Kate? The bicycle on the wall gave her pleasure. Shouldn't that stand for something? There had to be a balance between the giving and the keeping. Anything else was insane in a world like this one. Maybe it was time to think about buying instead of giving, but there was nothing she wanted anymore. Sitting in the water, letting her thoughts drain away because they were impure, she ran the shower. The shower spray pelting her in the tub was like rain on the ocean. She washed her hair in the rain, thick lather running down her neck. The giving was no longer optional. Anything else was a sin, a humiliation, and a selfish abomination that she could not tolerate. She understood it was time to let go of the bike.

She turned off the shower and stared at the gleaming silver faucet, as bright against white porcelain as the beam from a lighthouse. At her office, she managed six people who worked the phones, each one in a tiny cubicle. Each day passed like every other day, to the sound of six voices haranguing delinquents. Sometimes they read from scripts before them, as they were supposed to do. Sometimes they improvised. "When can we expect that first payment?" one said. "It's quite likely we can arrange a payback schedule to accommodate your situation and satisfy your debts. But we need a commitment to halt proceedings."

"Hey, I'm sorry about that cancer," one said. "You want us to repossess? Maybe that would be best? Easiest all the way around?"

"Look," one said, "I don't want to hear about it. When I hang up this phone, I want you to take out your checkbook and get that check in the mail. Otherwise, buddy, we'll see you in court. You think about that and I'll call back in fifteen minutes, a half an hour.

You're going to answer the phone when I call. And what are you going to say? What's that? No. You're going to say, 'Dave, the check is in the mail.' And tomorrow, or at the absolute latest the day after, your check is going to be here. In the mail, just like Zen Buddhism. That's the deal, buddy. Otherwise, I call you back. You make me call you back, I won't be so nice."

In her bedroom, lying down, very still, hands crossed neatly over the black-and-white stripes that covered her navel, chest rising and falling slightly with each breath, her sex itched and she thought about masturbating, even fondled herself a little, but at the moment there wasn't anyone she could imagine giving herself to. Her heartbeat had a kind of jangle to it. Sex, even imaginary sex, would make it worse. There was something wrong with her heart. She told herself to relax, crossed her hands again, and listened to one beat follow another. She could also hear water dripping. She counted droplets and thought about having it fixed. But a new washer would wear out and the aggravation would start up again, one slow droplet followed by two fast ones. Besides, the sound had a pattern. Her mood changed and the pattern of droplets repeating themselves hypnotized her into drowsy oblivion, as though a dripping faucet could be a path to nirvana, forgetfulness, not giving, not receiving. She dozed for a few minutes. Then she snapped awake, as she invariably did, heart beating madly, jangling again. Didn't she hear a jangle? Wouldn't a doctor call it a jangle, too? She was certain something was terribly, vaguely wrong. What was the matter? Or what mattered?

She had to take action. She knew that. If she waited, she would be punished. She had to give away the bicycle, pronto, not tomorrow, tonight, so she pulled on a pair of jeans, found her keys on a table next to a vase of drooping flowers and a bowl of stale fruit.

When she returned an hour later with a bicycle lock from the hardware store and a bottle of champagne, it was only for the bike. She put a red ribbon around its seat, attached the lock to the aluminum seat tube, and wheeled it around the room three or four times with a can of lubricating oil in one hand. Her heart was still jangling because she still had the bike and she had to give it away before Kate finished her evening shift. When she was certain that even a mechanic would cross his arms and stand back from the bike with a smile of satisfaction, she picked it up carefully so that nothing would come loose on the stoop or the front steps. She had the bottle of champagne tucked under one arm.

With the champagne like that, she made her way through moderate traffic to the debt-collection agency. She biked south and east, zigzagging with the blocks toward the lake, and there were times when her view of the Chicago skyline was unobstructed. At such times, gliding almost carelessly, things seemed more manageable; it looked as if the entire city could be taken in hand like a Tinkertoy. She started humming "He's Got the Whole World in His Hands."

At a red light, a man in a rusty-yellow pickup drinking from a half-pint bottle told her to throw her bike in back. He was wearing a black sweatshirt with a hood. The shirt had some team's logo printed on it. It looked like a bull. He told her he would give her a ride anywhere. She ignored him. He followed her, staying close. "Hey, honey," he said, pulling up as she pedaled, "you're God's gift. And me, honey? Today, I'm God!"

"Go away," she said. "I have a gun."

"Like hell you do." He snorted at the idea. "But I tell you what, sweetheart. I'll show you mine if you show me yours."

She swerved against traffic down a one-way street. By the time she reached the old, well-kept building where the agency was located, the underarms of her striped shirt were drenched in sweat and her hair smelled like exhaust. As she unlocked the front entranceway, the yellow pickup turned the corner and stopped at the curb. The driver saluted her with his half-pint bottle and honked his horn. The hood of his sweatshirt was pulled up around his face. She rolled the bicycle into the building, stood it on its kickstand, placed the bottle of champagne on the floor, and locked the door behind her.

She stood for a minute or so, catching her breath. A circular staircase in the middle of the vestibule separated a half dozen or so offices. Through the frosted glass of the debt-collection agency's door she could hear the muffled voices of solicitors. They were hounding delinquents, in some cases promising them they could "pay *and* play" until all their debts were dissolved and they were on the information highway to a worry-free future. Standing apart from the whole business, listening to the gimmicks from the lobby embarrassed her. It was the seesaw approach to debt collection. Almost all the solicitors were students or part-timers who came and went at horrific speed. Besides her, the exceptions were Dave, who was relentless, and Kate, whose bike had been stolen a week ago. Why hadn't she been told about it sooner? That would have made the giving easier.

Occasionally Dave's voice rose to an abrasive exclamation point. That was Dave all right, double-shift Dave, his harangues legendary; he harassed his deadbeats until they agreed to pay, whereupon he lavished praise upon them and promised, "as God is my witness," to make them creditworthy. Kate's voice, on the other hand, was always kind. She worked quietly, creating an upbeat rapport with people who had every reason to hate her. Over the phone they would tell her things they told nobody else, own up to any humiliation. Delinquents did not want to disappoint Kate.

After she locked the bike to a baluster, she leaned the champagne against the spokes of one wheel and sat on the stairs to write a note. In big, bold letters she addressed the envelope to Kate with a magic marker and put the key to the bicycle lock inside the envelope with the note, which she did not sign. Dave would recognize the bike, and she would have to depend upon him to keep her secret. They were entirely unsuited for one another, but she had told him a lot of things that nobody else knew after getting drunk one night and becoming his lover. Now she let him have his way, a condition she ascribed to the configuration of the stars.

She taped the envelope to the bicycle. As she rose to inspect her handiwork, the stairwell creaked loudly and she heard the jangle of keys. The night watchman, a bearded, heavyset man in his fifties, made his way down the stairs. As he advanced, his eyes for a moment glowed in the stairwell's dim light, but in the brighter glare of the lobby he turned brittle, as though losing bone mass. He wore a woolen shirt and a pair of dungarees held up by black suspenders. She wasn't certain if he saw her or not; his eyes had that dull, stupid glaze produced by incipient cataracts or extreme myopia. Even so, she felt found out in the middle of her solitary oblation, as though the bearded man was in her bedroom staring at her while she fondled herself.

"Today, he's God," she said, as though to explain her presence.

"God?" The watchman frowned. He lowered his gray beard into his collarbone, pulled up his eyebrows, and tilted his head. He seemed to think she was making him the butt of some joke. "Who?"

"The man who followed me here in a truck." Listening to Dave's voice lacerate another debtor, she knew that she would not tell him any more secrets. She wanted to hide somewhere, to see and listen without being seen. "Stop staring," she said.

"Staring? I can barely see you without my specs." He sat down heavily on the stairs and rubbed his eyes. "God? I never heard of God cruising around in a truck."

"He was wearing a hood."

"A hood? God." The watchman clipped his ring of keys to a belt loop and reached into a pocket for his eyeglasses. He held them at a distance from his eyes, studying the lenses, bifocal and very thick, and shaking his head. He finally put on the glasses and peered through the balusters. "I do not believe," he said, speaking deliberately, "that I have ever had a day when I thought I was God." His eyes were owlish in their black frames. He took off his glasses and pinched his nose.

She could hear his heavy, labored breathing and Dave's voice, rising to a frenzied pitch through the frosted glass. She shifted her weight. The floor creaked. He reached between the balusters and stroked the bicycle's seat, the seat that reminded her of a cow's skull. "You know something about her bike? What happened to it, I mean?"

She closed her eyes and felt herself sway. "I'm giving her my bike."

"So, you get to be God, too." The watchman put his glasses back on. "Who else gets to be God?" He stared fiercely, eyebrows arched. It's something he could say to the president, she thought, to the kids down the block who sat on the stoop of a bombed-out building selling crack cocaine with their Raiders caps turned backward.

"Look, you want that champagne? Kate's getting a bike. That's plenty."

"I work here. You don't have to give me anything."

"Why not? You don't drink?"

Dave came through the door and discovered the two of them, the bicycle and the note. "Well, well, well," he said, "what have we here?" He winked at her, and soon enough had Kate and the other workers gathered in an approximate circle around the watchman, the gift giver, and the gift.

"Kate," she said, "I want you to have this bicycle." A silence descended upon the circle. Even Dave shut up. "It's a good bicycle," she said. "It'll take you anywhere you want to go." She glanced from Kate, who stared quietly at her, to the bicycle, which filled the room like a symphony, to the night watchman, who seemed to be enjoying himself, massaging the arthritic knuckles of his liver-spotted hands and peering at the proceedings. There was a connection, some sense of kinship between her and the younger woman and the older man that she could not put into words. It was as though someone invisible had entered the room and enclosed the three of them in an envelope of air where ESP was possible.

Kate hugged her and thanked her extravagantly. The spell was broken. Dave ordered everyone back to his or her station except for Kate. He popped open the champagne and took a swig. He tried to put his arm around his lover, but she stiffened and frowned. Dave shrugged. He passed the bottle to Kate, who smiled happily. "Cool," Kate said. "Way cool."

A minute later, back in the street, Patricia hailed a taxi. "Take me home," she said to the driver and gave him the address. She stared behind her into the street. "Some guy is after me."

"Story of your life, huh, lady? No problem," the taxi driver said. "Be happy. Don't worry." He was Asian; she decided he was

Vietnamese because he smiled sweetly through the sliding panel of plastic that separated him from her. She drummed her nails nervously on the plastic. She felt like she was riding in a police car after an accident.

"Story of my life? What do you mean?"

"Joke," the driver said. "*Ha. Ha.* Story of your life." He squinted at her, smiled again, then turned decisively and jerked the vehicle into gear. She wondered whether he was drunk, but soon enough buildings blurred past—the driver was good, whipping through traffic, avoiding lights—and she thought about the bicycle like a friend she would miss. She leaned forward against the plastic panel and stared at the lights on the dashboard, curious about the driver, but his ID card was nowhere in sight. Wasn't that irregular? "What's your name?" she said. "Are you Vietnamese? You legal?"

He said nothing. The yellow light from some sort of electronic device gave his face an eerie glow and she saw that the cab had a radio and asked the driver to tune it to Chicago's gospel music station. He obliged her. "Go Down Moses" was playing.

There was a small brass bell on the front seat next to him. "Where did the bell come from?" she asked, but the driver didn't hear her above the music. He seemed to be nodding his head to the rhythm of the gospel. She pointed and tapped on the plastic, certain that the greasy, blackened bell had once belonged to her and given her a jolt of human connection whenever she struck it. It was so palpable, so lived with, and so different from her fictional insubstantiality that she wanted to reach out and cling to its simple wooden handle. "The bell," she said. "Where did you get it?"

The driver stared into the mirror. He reached behind him and slid open the plastic panel. "You know such a thing?" he said. "Must be reason for it, you know? I find out, I *let* you know. Now I leave it here, just in case. I'm, what you say, ready?" He glanced in the mirror and rubbed the back of his neck.

"Why don't you drive along the lake?" she said. "Take me down Michigan Avenue, make a circle past the fountain. Can you do that for me?"

He grunted and veered into the change lane. As he maneuvered onto the Outer Drive, heading south for the Chicago skyline, away from where she lived, she became convinced that he needed to know more about her. She told him that she had once had in her basement many tapes of gospel choirs and charismatic Southern preachers, all inherited from her father, and that sometimes, bereft, she had locked herself down there with a boom box and a jug of wine and listened all night to the tapes, baritones promising salvation and sweet-voiced choirs singing out their sorrow and belief. "I only wanted to touch the bell," she said. "It's the first thing I've really wanted to touch in a long time."

The radio played "Nobody Knows the Trouble I've Seen."

He squealed to a stop. "I take you home now," he said. He did not seem unfriendly. "You come up front, hold bell."

Horns blared behind him. Someone shouted out an obscenity. She sat against the door with the greasy bell in her lap and they started moving again. He kept driving toward the Chicago skyline, the Miracle Mile, and it made her feel lucky, as though she was going somewhere on her own, pedaling through traffic on the bicycle. She could see the Hancock Tower. It looked self-important and grandiose. Soon enough, she knew, the lake would disappear from sight and they would be beneath it. The city would swallow her up.

"Marry me," he said. "You make me legal, no hanky-panky. Then you keep bell." He reached over and touched her arm. "Will you marry me?"

"Marry you?" she said. She could feel the solid weight of his proposal holding her down; it was exactly as heavy as the bell in her lap. He looked about her age, with fine wrinkles around his eyes and hair the color of steel filings. In the close air of the taxi, his life was like the lake tonight, smooth and glassy. He owned his life. It had a history that was true and not false. He came from a place that she could only imagine, but his village reality was as brassy and vivid as the blackened bell. It meant something to him and he would keep it as long as he could. She had given away everything, and maybe everything had been taken from him, but either way she was still left over. He was still left over. That was at least a start. That was history.

As she waited, poised and expectant to hear what she might say, she struck the bell. She struck it tentatively at first and its high chime surprised her, like a late-night caller at the door. She slammed it against her palm, dulling the clean sound, then banged it twice against the window, a kind of clanging noise, but thereafter rang it the way it was meant to be rung, like pedaling a bicycle, with a full-throated peal that rang out over the gospel loud and clean, like something worth keeping for as long as she could.

SUDDENLY I MEET YOUR FACE

Robert's studio was a mess, full of bits and pieces of other people. He worked with a blowtorch, put fire to bones and objects. A plastic fork from a fast-food joint, Astroturf from the local football field, slate found mysteriously on the abandoned railroad tracks. Cigarette butts, the housing from a shattered electric clock. He used chicken bones because he worked the graveyard shift in a local diner, cleared away bones in fluorescent glare. He laminated everything biodegradable in clear plastic to make it last.

The woman with the studio next to his was a performance artist. Because she used a syringe, there were protests about her performances, about the bloodletting in the streets. The medical establishment disapproved. An antiobscenity crusader used her name in vain. One day, taking coffee with Robert, she looked around his workplace, her dark hair floating near her face as though it was conscious. "You have any plans for that syringe, that dirty gauze? I have to pull together a performance piece for an uptown club," she said, "and it looks like you've got a lot of medical waste here."

She leaned over his table and traced a coffee ring with a long, slender finger. Her eyes narrowed and Robert's face turned salty and hot. Everything she did was perfect. She was wearing cutoffs, rested a fine swell of calf on the sun-roasted skin above her other knee, the place where her thighs curved together. She had perfect legs. "Blood stays stable at room temperature for at least a week," she told Robert, and wrinkled up her nose. "Come with me."

She had a lilting Southern way of walking, a little heavy with sexual promise. Robert liked to imagine she had to balance her sexual weight against the blood she let. Walking into her space on a bright sunlit afternoon was instant trauma, like having a heart attack and being wheeled into the Day-Glo glare of a hospital operating room. White floor, white walls, white table, the whole place white except for a long sloping skylight and black curtain between their two studios. On her worktable—a solid lacquered slab of oak—a compound microscope had a camera attached to it. She took Kodacolor photographs of drops of blood on a slide, blew them up, and hung them with shining clamps from wires.

Test tubes of her blood were carefully arranged in stainless steel racks. *Jimmy Wong's Club, spring equinox; under the El at Wabash, summer solstice; uptown Broadway, feast of Michaelmas.* Black-and-white photographs were thumbtacked to the wall above each rack. Plastic tubes snaked from an arm, the glare of sunlight baked into asphalt.

She motioned to the microscope. Things swam in there. Corpuscles, plasma, never the same river twice. "We think it's what we expect from life," she said. "But it's the other way around, isn't it?" Her cells grew flaccid in test tubes, decomposed in full view. Robert circled the neighborhood, the whole city, wandered until his soles wore through, but for her a breakthrough was as close as the pressure in their arteries, if their devotion to art and each other was perfect.

"You don't shoot up, do you?" she said.

"No. No." A white rotating fan on her worktable cut into the wet heat. "No. Do you?"

"I don't put things in there," she said, rubbing the crook of her arm, "I take things out." She nodded to the microscope. "You like what's inside of me?"

Robert turned salty again. He had been alone for what seemed like a long time. Listen to your heart, he wanted to say, listen to my blood, listen to your blood, and listen to my heart.

His motto was, When the heart breaks, the body heals.

There was a bead of sweat on her forehead where she parted her hair. Her mouth was a little crooked, as though grinning aloud, and she reached for a legal pad. "Let's reevaluate the artistic significance of medical waste."

Everything was so white, so dazzling, her eyes so intense above the intricate precision of the microscope, that Robert rose out of his body, as though staring through a camera that circled them, and climbed into her body through the test tubes around them, like getting into the secret eye of the eye, the one nobody knows about. He breathed her blood and smothered himself in her lungs. They were moving instead of the camera. It was one of those moments when everything becomes clear. Her nose tilted away from a dark spot on her upper lip. Her face grew smaller, then ballooned and pulsated inches from Robert. One of her freckled arms grazed a test tube of blood. She balanced it against the microscope. "Blood brothers," she said, leaning forward and touching the dimple on Robert's right cheek.

They left each other notes. Robert gave up chicken bones, paid attention to gestures, small shifting moods. She was a real live person who liked to move her arms in the lamplight at night and make crazy shadows on the ceiling. She was her own kind of mess, he came to see, not perfect at all. They spent hours each day with her blood. They could have been married. They were mostly quiet, like laboratory assistants, but he told her things, she let him see an unhappy cloistered childhood and lovers who had all turned sour. Robert would walk from the all-night diner, all the chicken, into the bright glare of *Blood Cells: A Performance Piece*. His blood ached for her at night, but still something pulled them apart. They quarreled over the piece, which was mostly blood, mostly hers. She wanted everything her way. He had to give up his objects, the bits and pieces he made a life out of, but she got to keep everything, and him to boot. Robert developed the idea that his life was ending, that nothing but risk mattered.

At the diner one night, she showed up in a skintight crimson dress and a blond wig. She munched french fries, her eyes gleaming. "Suddenly I meet your face," she said to Robert, and licked her lips before sashaying out the door.

"Burn, baby, burn," a drunk at the counter said. Two others stumbled out the door trying to follow her.

Robert tried to take her to the abandoned railroad tracks, where they might find some slate, but she teased him instead into a medical supply house. They purchased culture tubes with screw caps, a beaker, a burner, clamps, a thermometer, and tongue depressors. Robert walked off, face hard, then came back. "So you love me?" she said, squinting and bringing her face close to his.

"Burn, baby, burn," he said quietly, imitating the drunk because he felt drunk and lost in the bright glare.

She gave up studio cutoffs and black leather vests for a red cotton blouse and a navy blue skirt, as though on leave from parochial school, but it was her idea, not his. He wanted her to wear something white. "This isn't about purity," she said, rinsing blood from her hands.

They transported the studio wholesale to the uptown club, down to the test tubes of blood and notepads full of scrawled choreography. Photographs were arranged in patterns, walls painted Day-Glo white.

By the night of the performance, a wet Friday when neon echoed like music, Robert's solitary forays into the city in search of found objects were history, of a time when he could outtalk his fat, never-ending lust. He was losing weight, feeling feverish. Secretly he took antibiotics.

Familiar faces wandered into the club, folded up umbrellas, and grabbed folding chairs. A carousel of slides projected blood cells magnified a thousand times. The raucous sound of a crow squawked from the club's speakers. Her old lovers were part of the program, a Polish guy who had disappeared from her life for weeks at a time and a painter she had lived with for two years. That relationship had ended one afternoon in a large white room when he told her to leave. He sat in the back row, fretting with his invitation. Robert wanted to know why he had come. Robert wanted to know why he was invited. When the painter had left her, he had told her he didn't believe in monogamy, but had practiced it for her sake. The breakup wasn't her fault, he told her, no, not at all; she was beautiful, immensely talented. She would come to see his decision to leave was best for all concerned. He wasn't the kind of man who could live with one woman, especially a woman who was perfect. After he left her, she went a little crazy. There were one-night stands at art colonies where she retreated after the painter sent her away. There was an affair with an Oakland artist who recited mantras and projected nature slides as they made it. One day he hit her, not much, but she bled. Sticky and gelatinous, inky. Art absolutely personal, public art, too, history and presence together, a museum to the rhythms of the heart.

Most of this was contained in the program an usher in black tails gave out at the door, along with a pamphlet, condoms, and bleach kits. This story is the performance, Robert wrote in the program, who I am, or who I pretend to be, and what's the difference? And on the program were scribbles she had made in her version of Robert's own hand. Her hand, writing, pretending to be Robert's hand. "Forget everything but blood. My blood is alive with promise. Blood, when burned, merges, blood mergers for a new millennium. Always refreshing, never mechanical, even when produced by mechanical reproduction."

A wave machine spurted water, dyed red, across the canvas that covered the floor. Microphones dangled from the ceiling and the audience dared not even whisper, fearing exposure. Her ex-lovers raised their feet and sat cross-legged. On a video, a sailboat with black-and-white sails and a blood-red life preserver headed out to sea. Even if modified, Robert said, the lights dimming, blood has its reasons, its ways. People who die on account of blood should never be surprised.

"Rage!" said her amplified voice, followed by the sound of a crow, then by the drone of a gamelan, an assortment of chants, drumbeats, bamboo flutes. *People who die on account of blood should say, Pay it no never mind,* she scrawled across a poster.

"Rage!" Robert shouted.

"Witness me, vanishing!" she screamed back.

"I am one of you, but this is *my* untainted blood," Robert said.

"Rage!" she shouted.

"I'm everyone, I'm nobody, I'm everywhere, I'm nowhere," Robert said.

"Rage!"

"Witness us, vanishing," Robert said.

"Rage!"

"What part of you unknown to me has become part of me?" Robert asked.

"Rage!"

"How much of my blood once it leaves my body tells the truth about me?" Robert asked.

"Rage!"

"What if you test my blood?"

"Rage!"

"Will it hold true to who I am?"

"Rage!"

"Or is my blood fiction?"

"Rave on!"

She unbuttoned her blouse and skirt. Lights clicked on above two chicken-bone totems. A dream catcher hung between the totems. The dream catcher, complete with illegal bird feathers, was above an imprint of Robert's hand.

She stood in a bra, white panties, and fishnet stockings, one leg hitched on a chair. She hummed "Lili Marlene." A spotlight descended until it was inches above the table, illuminating only her torso and an inch of thigh between the fishnet stockings and the panties. The light cut off her head. She found a vein, inserted the syringe, and filled it with blood. She squirted the blood into a ceramic bowl. A large mirror was positioned above the bowl. The audience saw blood glisten.

She gave Robert the syringe, as though a conversation of vital importance finally was reaching its climax. Robert stripped down to his jockey shorts and stood, love handles and all.

"The major blood-exchange risk now is among drug users who

share needles," she said. "The next step is inevitable, like forgetting to use a condom in the heat of passion." She nodded and Robert, making a fist, drew blood, thinking of the corpuscles squirming on the slide. He squirted the blood into the bowl, placed the syringe on a patch of dirty gauze beside it, and invited the audience to participate, with or without bleach kits.

"Official history may be too important to leave to politicians," she said. "These are revolutionary times." To the high-pitched squawk of the crow, she moved close and French-kissed Robert, then lifted the porcelain bowl. Each took a sip.

"Do this in memory of me," she said.

Two men dressed in black came forward. Each dipped a finger in the bowl of blood and made a sign of the cross, touching forehead, heart, and both collarbones.

The audience filed out quietly, according to the instructions on the program, and Robert, embarrassed in the normal light, made a pledge to jog off his love handles. He walked her home in light drizzle, the streets still glistening, pockmarked with dimples. She could still be perfect, he pretended, the woman he imagined when the black curtain separated them, when they were coffee companions, making each other up as they went along. Later, after they made love, he thought about wandering again, stumbling upon old linoleum tiles or battered toasters, spent condoms or splintered tongue depressors, all those things people mislay or give up or toss out. There was no purity in what he found, and perhaps not even much purity in what he made of it, but her blood was her blood, not his. He was conspiring already with the bits and pieces of the world that would somehow attach themselves to him.

Time looped forward to a day when he entered a clinic and had his blood tested, just to make sure. By then she had already found herself in another lover, so nothing they did permanently damaged them, and it didn't much change them either. At least, Robert's motto didn't change, though his constructions became memorials, jagged wood pieces with charred bones attached, like crosses salting the land. But that night they were still tasting each other like hot peppers burning the tongue. Her fingers followed his vein from the wrist to the crook of the arm, where she stopped. She went round and round the punctured spot, round and round, not certain how to proceed, because after that his blood was secret again.

CATCH AND RELEASE

It was one of those days when the sky is the color of cement; it played havoc with my bipolar disorder. A storm watch was in place and the radio said it would be a bad one. It was cold out, too, below the donut, so I drove quick from my hospital job and parked close to the discount store next to a flatbed truck loaded with lumber. I was standing next to my pickup, locking its door, when people burst from the store's gunmetal exits in shock like the septic ones at the hospital. They waved their arms and screamed into the cement clouds. Some dragged their coats in the snirt—that's snow mixed with dirt. Some had the bottom of their faces covered with paper towels.

I didn't know if it was a bomb or a monster or what.

A cop with a bullhorn was speaking to people inside the store. "Come out with your hands up!" he shouted. It was a movie. I was excited. It was really something. I looked for the cameras and lights.

A man beside me, breathing hard, rested a hand on the lumber in the flatbed and studied the scene. I fumbled my keys and bent down to get them and when I stood up again, he was staring my way, giving me the once-over.

"So what's all the excitement about?" I said brightly. "A sale?" He had himself a nice beveled head of hair, which I noticed because it was too cold to be without a hat, and he had a nice crease on either side of his mouth. He looked to me like a good piece of wood.

"Aerosol cans. Men with aerosol cans," he said. "Still Life with Aerosol Cans."

"Ah," I said. So it was a plot, I thought; that explained the wail of the ambulance and the blue lights and the cops sealing off every exit. I liked how he said it, too, as if he had put the words inside a picture frame on my living room wall. I'm divorced, you know, so I'm always working at it, trying to beat back the monsters if I meet a man who might be worth reeling in.

We call it catch and release where I come from.

Besides, I'm a sucker for beveled hair.

I got talking and found out the flatbed truck with all that lumber belonged to him. It looked like enough wood for a room. A nice four-season room on the back of my house. And it wasn't loblolly that could grow only in the swamp and had to be imported, it was hardwood. I could tell it might stay true.

I squinted into the cement sky. "Damn," I said. "Aerosol cans. That sure is something. What do you make of that?"

He ran his gloved fingers through that gorgeous hair, mussing himself a bit. "I write some of them poems, you know, so I think I might make a poem out of it. 'Men with Aerosol Cans,' I might call it." He smiled and looked away from me. He said something else, but a helicopter whirled overhead and muffled his words.

"You make poems," I said after the noise faded "That is really something. That sure is something." I didn't think much of it, actually, but this is the reason a lie works better than the truth with a man. Sooner or later, even standing in cold below the donut, they tell me what they own and where they work. And if they do something like make poems, well, you better believe I'm going to hear about that. They try to convince me that they're the cat's pajamas and I'm the cat. That's when human nature kicks in and I lie. I make up a story to keep them busy so I can look and not listen.

"Want me to recite them for you?" he said.

"Recite poems? Out here? In the cold?" I said. "Are you kidding? Aren't there better places to do that kind of thing?" Maybe if I was still in high school, I thought. If you have to do it at all, I thought. I mean, there's plenty of poets in high school. That's a place for poets, I thought, high school. After that, a man would do better to learn some practical thing, like construction or car mechanics. Poems are just words, though I suppose you can lie when you make them up and that might be another way to beat back the monster.

But poet or not, he still had that gorgeous head of beveled hair. I wanted to get my hands in there and muss it myself, so I bit my tongue. At least he's different, I thought.

I've gone through four and you betcha the fifth won't be like them others.

"Ah, the cold," he said. "I didn't think of that. You see, I'm immune."

"From the cold?" I said.

"Yes, that's right." He ran a gloved hand through his hair again and I tell you, it was really something to see. I stopped thinking about the cold. I just wanted to get him in bed. Don't let them feminists fool you; we women always think like that when we find a man we want.

"You know," he said, "there's a bar just across the street. I could do with a drink. Like to join me?"

I squinted to indicate I was thinking about it. I took off my gloves and bit one of my fingers and looked down at the snirt. Looked down demurely. Men like that kind of thing, you know, especially a man with a mind kept over from high school.

Across the parking lot, one of the cops shouted into his bullhorn. The helicopter whirled around the perimeter of the building. I would not have been surprised if someone had shouted "Action!" and a famous actor had stepped from the shadows. Finally, when I saw him get antsy like he might go have that drink by himself, I smiled my brightest smile. I don't mind telling you that my smile is something to see. In high school, it was voted the best in my class. "Yes," I said, "a drink would be lovely."

It's a word I save and use sparingly; you betcha it did the job real good this time. He took my elbow so I wouldn't go slipping, you know, and looked out for me the way a man like him needs to do, though I was the one with the Canadian boots and he was the one wearing pigskin oxfords.

Even though the light was heavy outside, inside the bar it was liquid and dark and crowded with people, many of them fugitives from the attack of the aerosol can vandals. A stocky farmer in overalls with a flushed face was telling his story in a loud voice. He was often interrupted. "No," someone would say, "you're remembering it all wrong." "Devil with that," the farmer said. "Listen again, brother. I was there. I saw the man." And he started over from the top.

A cop took down notes. Every so often his walkie-talkie burped out static.

"Did that guy say he saw the man?" the poet said. He turned to me with a strange exalted light in his eyes. "Salt of the earth," he said. "These are my people. I call them flatlanders in my new series of poems. I like to come to a place like this and sit in the corner in a booth close enough to the bartender to hear everything he says. Let's sit down so I can write a poem."

Good grief, I thought, but I said, "Yes, let's do that, that would be lovely, just lovely," and I smiled. He got the gist of what I said, but he missed the tone entirely. Him and me settled into a booth, though not in the corner, and I excused myself to powder my nose. When I got back, he had taken off his gloves and ordered me a half-liter of burgundy, which I like but can't drink unless I take my antihistamines. I took a sip of it anyway and licked my lips, which I don't mind saying are scrumptious. He was staring at them wistfully and I knew I had already pulled him from the water and had him in the boat. But did I want to keep him or let him go?

"Say something," he said.

"Lovely," I said and made the word last a long time.

He motioned to the small crowd still standing near the door with glasses of Grain Belt beer in their hands. "Do you mind if I listen and take notes? I always like to put some real detail in my poems."

"A poet," I said, and smiled, though by this time my hundred-tooth smile was getting a bit glassy. Even so, I nodded as though I was amazed. "That sure is something," I said. But it was a lie. I was beginning to have my doubts. He was scribbling away in an itty-bitty notebook like a gambler figuring out his debts. How could he write a real poem if he told the truth and copied down the things people said while they got drunk? He'll just give himself away, whoever he is. In high school, I thought, the real poet was the one who could lie the best, the one who believed his lie but knew he was lying, at least to himself.

I know how to lie and how to look at things. Maybe I was the one who should be the poet.

I felt sad and I can't blame it on my bipolar disorder. This poet fish was not going to swim that night in my bed, I could tell, and I packed up my rod and reel, put away my favorite bait, and yanked the rope on my outboard to get back to shore. I had reeled him in, but now I was ready to put him back. That beveled head of his that I had so much wanted to touch would still have every strand in place come morning. He was so lost in whatever he was writing that he didn't even notice the way my mood changed; he just kept scribbling in that itty-bitty book and making faces and picking his teeth with his tongue. It was not a pretty sight, I can tell you. I let my mind wander and sipped the vino, too much of it maybe, and started feeling drowsy and said good-bye to the four-season room that he was supposed to build for me so I could sit through the worst winter and look at everything, everything.

I started feeling a little mean. When I squinted back across the booth in the bad light, he was staring at me with tears in his eyes. "I finished my poem," he said.

"Read it to me," I said. "But not just to me. To every one of us here. We all deserve to hear it." I was only kidding, sort of, in a mean kind of way, and I would have apologized to him if he had called my bluff, but instead he started reading in a slow voice, at first to me alone. Once he moved himself to tears, I motioned to him like a conductor in a school band and got him to stand up in the booth. "Go on, climb up on the table so we can all hear it," I said. "You've been wanting to do this for a long time. A damn long time. Go for it. Do it. Grab for the gusto." And he did it. He climbed up on the table so everyone could see his oxfords and his white socks.

I shouted, "Hey everyone, this guy is going to read us a poem! He's a goddamn poet!"

Still Life with Aerosol Cans

Today there are storm warnings.
The Wife is at home dying of thirst.
This is my secret, brother: I have an aerosol can
I keep in the back of my truck.
I'm the Unabomber of the Prairie!
I like to spray and spray and spray.
If I rage and rage in the dying light
of the Wal-Mart store, if I mistake
my aerosol can for a typewriter,
I might not make it home by morning.
Friend, how much are those pickled eggs?

We all stared speechless until he climbed back down, a little red-faced, into the booth. "Drinks on the house!" he shouted. "On me!" A couple of customers came over and slapped him on the back. A couple of others gave him squirmy looks, paid their tabs, and left the bar fast.

"You know you borrowed that last line verbatim from that guy in overalls?" I said.

"That's all right," he said, "except I don't borrow, I steal."

He was quite pleased with himself until the cop thought twice about what he had just heard and came over to the booth to invite the poet outside so that the two of them could take a look at that truck of his with the aerosol can in back. That was it for the poet; he walked out the door and out of my life, his face drained of color, and I recalled how hard he had been breathing standing next to his lumber truck.

I grew curious about what the cop might find in the truck, but not curious enough to go see for myself. Instead, I drank my fill of wine and picked up his pencil, which still lay on the table across from me. I turned his notebook every which way, thinking how strange it was, and then, a word at a time, I rewrote his poem, the darnedest thing for me to do. I did it just to see if I could beat back the monster, not with a man but with words, with the way they lie on the page if you stare long enough.

Today, I wrote, the truth

> is like snirt,
> undrinkable, each of us dying of thirst
> and it's all over the country
> covering everything without distinction.

That was pretty good, I thought, and I waved to the bartender for another half-liter of that good, red stuff. The histamines became like little brain bugs that had been dormant for years. My bipolar began to rage. I understood that I could spend the rest of the day woodworking the poems until they had a certain shape to them. Once I got them right, each one in turn, I could mail him the whole shebang. That would be something, I thought, a poetess outpoeting a poet. I settled back in the booth, tucked a foot under a thigh, used my elbows to shield my construction work from scrutiny, and let the words have their way with me.

MOVEMENT OF NATURAL LIGHT

John Bloor and his stepson, Hammer, bought the aquarium several months before they moved from California to the Chicago suburbs. They stocked it with dwarf angels, damselfish, clown fish, and a large butterfly, a predatory creature the clerk at the high-tech pet store told Bloor could be trouble. Bloor liked the risk factor, he told his wife, Phoebe, who stood over them as they assembled the tank. "Imagine damsels and butterflies terrorizing an angel," he said, his mouth just a little crooked.

"John," she said skeptically, "why now?" She was wearing a black embroidered sweater and her hair was pulled back tightly. "Why not when we get to Wilmette? It's just something else to take apart. I'm very tired of taking things apart. It's just another breakable object to move."

"This is the time. You'll see why," he said, motioning her away. He did in fact have an answer to her question, and it concerned Hammer. He wanted his stepson to be a normal child who ate hot dogs, played baseball, and thought a lot about girls, and the aquarium was a first step, one initiated by Hammer. "John," he had said that morning, rousting his stepfather from sleep, "let's go get my aquarium. You've been promising it for months."

Hammer, old enough to decide he was a Buddhist, donated a rotund stone figure to the aquarium. It was about the size of a large egg, and the pygmy angel, in particular, took to it immediately, nibbling on it, keeping it clean of algae. Bloor, as a child strictly a Catholic, now a nothing, chuckled indulgently. "Buddha belongs in a fish tank."

"When it happens, it happens in a flash," Hammer said, and added, too enigmatically for Bloor's taste, "Now the fish can nibble on the pearls that were his eyes."

Phoebe liked the aquarium. Late in the evening, she often sat in its light, the rest of the room dark, its coral shining, the "Symphony of Sorrowful Songs" playing on the stereo. "It's beautiful and sad at the same time," she said, sipping her nightcap, wearing a gown with a scalloped silk collar that Bloor liked to feel between his fingertips. "Sometimes it looks like Disneyland, sometimes like Kubla Khan's pleasure dome."

"Pleasure dome," repeated Bloor. He let the words roll around in his mouth. "Disneyland."

"It's a miracle of rare device," Phoebe said, putting down her drink and leaning against Bloor, who stiffened a little before putting his arm around her and reaching for the collar. "It's wonderful when we connect, isn't it? It happens so seldom."

"Connect," said Bloor, sipping his own drink and nodding a little as he stared into the tank.

- - - - -

"When we get to Wilmette," Bloor told her later, folding his *Wall Street Journal* and tossing it beside the bed, "I'd like to send Hammer to a real school, one with a baseball team."

"A baseball team?" Phoebe let her mouth stay a little open. She closed her book and tilted her head toward him, as though to hear well.

"A baseball team, a cafeteria that serves red meat." Bloor ticked off the items and stared at his stubby fingers. "You know, regular *stuff*. Great Books. A yearbook, a high school ring. Calculus. Stuff he can use. I mean, there's nothing wrong with meditation, biofeedback, yoga, and tofu, all that crap. I'm just saying the boy has his spiritual foundation, maybe now it's time to take him away from the yoga school."

"It's not a 'yoga school'. It's an institute of personal transformation."

"Whatever." Bloor smirked. "Look, baby, no reason to call me names. I'm not trying to fight or anything. I'm just making a sensible suggestion." He nodded sagely in his pajamas and stared at the star-patterned quilt. "I just think he needs some *real* education."

In her nightgown, seductive and slinky, she stalked to the bathroom door and turned. "Is there *anything* I do that you agree with?"

"Hey, I didn't mean to upset you. Come here, I'll show you something I like." Bloor saw the expression on her face change. He raised his eyebrows and grinned boyishly. "Hey, sorry. I didn't mean that. I'm teasing. We're just failing to communicate here, that's all."

She slammed the door. "Our problem has nothing to do with failure." Her voice was muffled, as though in the basin.

Bloor counted to ten. He forced himself to his feet, pulled up his sagging pajamas, and trudged to the closed door. "There just isn't a big demand for yogis, is there?" he said. "That's the only point I'm making."

Phoebe opened the door and stood there, arms crossed, steam still rising from the basin. "There's always two stories, John, there's always your story and the story of what's really going on."

Bloor, whose first marriage ended in muffled irreconcilable anger, nodded and pulled up his pajamas again. "You know what happened in front of that aquarium, Phoebe? We connected," he said, holding the pajamas in place with one hand. He launched into a negotiation strategy learned in business school and taken to heart.

Phoebe relaxed a little, dropping her arms. Bloor reached out to her. "I'm sorry," he said, and tried to kiss her. She turned away, so he pecked her on the cheek, a patronizing kiss, and offered a backrub. "Sometimes it's easier, and wiser," he said, his fingers working her spine, "to walk away from an argument. Will you just do me one favor?" His fingers dug in deep. "Will you just think about what I said?"

"All right," she mumbled. After a few minutes she sighed.

Satisfied, he told her about the angelfish, talking to himself when her breathing deepened to the rhythm of sleep.

In the morning, without his usual complaints, he drove Hammer to the yoga school. "You know," he said, "in high school I was a pitcher. I had a curve that nearly snapped off my arm at the elbow. I could be wild, but when I had control, man, I was something. They'd chase pitches already in the dirt. When I was good, son, I was *good.* You hear what I'm saying?"

"Loud and clear." Hammer formed a steeple with long, thin fingers over what looked like a roll of hospital gauze. "I don't believe in competition." He pursed his lips. "But I like the aquarium a lot. I just hope the tank is big enough. I'd hate to see that angel get eaten." He unwound the gauze and twined it around his head. "Tell me," he said, "did you ever go to church?"

Bloor, a little startled by the question, glanced at his stepson, who seemed quite curious, so he choked off an impatient, angry reply. "Yeah, I used to go to church. Every Sunday. Holy days, too. I was brought up Catholic."

"Did you pray?"

"Pray?" Bloor said ruefully. "Yeah, actually. All the time. Every night I'd say the Jesus Prayer a hundred times to make up for my sins. 'Lord Jesus Christ, have mercy on my soul.' I'd say the damn thing over and over. It didn't make me a better person, but it made me feel better about my sins."

"Why did you stop?"

"I don't know," he said tersely. "I got older. Other things became more important." Bloor had a scary feeling that took him back to the curtained confessional of his youth, so that the role of father and stepson was temporarily reversed. Bloor was the penitent, Hammer the father confessor.

"You ever think of going back?"

"To church, you mean?" he said gruffly. "No."

"I like to meditate in front of the aquarium. Would you ever try that with me?"

"I think not," Bloor said. If Hammer is the father confessor, then that makes the fish the church and the aquarium the sacrament, or maybe the aquarium is the church and the ocean the sacrament. Bloor played around with the notion, vaguely remembering some scripture, something about fish learned in Saturday morning catechism thirty years ago.

Hammer left it at that and Bloor kept his thoughts to himself. The rest of the way to school, Hammer tapped the dashboard and pointed out the neighborhood's "power points," places where a jogger could stop and breathe green healing energy. "You ought to run every afternoon. It would strengthen your resolve and improve your spirits."

"My resolve is just fine, thank you." Bloor smiled at the thought of himself jogging, his modest paunch jiggling like a pot roast. He braked to a stop at the school, a low-slung building without windows. The novice yogis, turbans wrapped tight, were meditating stone-faced on the lawn. "Son, it's all chemicals. We're pieces of meat. Dead meat, unless we're a little careful. That's what I believe these days. So keep control, sure, but throw a few curves along the way. Keep people guessing."

"That's really a depressing thing to say, Dad." Hammer opened the door. "Look at it this way." Dusty, unconditioned air rushed into the car. "We do what our karma demands." He closed the door and was shielded from any possible reply.

- - - - -

Phoebe and Hammer moved to Wilmette several weeks ahead of Bloor. He called each day. Had the fish survived the journey? Did the stress trigger any aggression in the large damsel? What about those bottom-dwelling gobies? The clown fish? Hammer reassured him on all counts, but Phoebe couldn't take him seriously. "You identify with that clown fish, don't you? Makes sense," she said, and laughed. "As for the stress, we've got two of them in therapy. They're coming along very nicely, thank you." Bloor was furious at her bantering tone and gave her strict instructions concerning the care and feeding of the fish. She and Hammer would be strictly responsible for their nurturing until he got to town.

"Yes sir," she said curtly. "Any other commands, your highness?"

She parked his Mercedes at O'Hare. His plane landed in an afternoon shower. He claimed his car and reached his new house after a long drive down moist suburban avenues. The trim was the color of the ocean, he thought. From the moment he climbed aboard the plane, he had daydreamed of his arrival, a wife waiting in the drive, a son on summer vacation with lots of time for his father, and the splendid peace of the aquarium.

At the front entranceway, Phoebe was unbraiding her hair and introducing Hammer to their new neighbor. "John, you're late," she said, flirtatious. Dappled by leaves, in playful sunlight, she was beautiful, and Bloor, rubbing his five o'clock shadow, asked himself an awkward question: Why am I aging so much faster than my wife is?

"I'm not late, just bewildered," he said, glancing at the new neighbor's curb, where bags of garbage had accumulated like sacks of leaves. The neighbor, a lean and hungry-looking Ron West, held out his hand and laughed. "The garbage collectors are on strike. I'm afraid, in fact, that one of our quick-tempered citizens ran over two of them while they were picketing." Phoebe stretched in her skimpy summer blouse. "It's tempting," West said, blue eyes sparkling, "to solve problems like that, in a flash."

Hammer studied the neighbor with interest, Bloor noticed. He felt a little flustered, diminished again by that odd feeling of being possessed by his childhood. He could swear that West had maliciously glanced at his waist and eyed his wife. "You've got some spittle on your chin."

West, goggle-eyed, stared at him. "Beg your pardon?"

"Spittle," Bloor said. "It's dripping down your chin." He pulled out a handkerchief and offered it to his neighbor.

West left quickly, his face flushed, and Phoebe was quietly furious. Bloor followed her to the couch. Scowling and tense, as angular as a piece of modern sculpture, she sat facing the aquarium. A lemon peel angel flickered against the glass, alternately visible and invisible in the movement of natural light.

"I'm sorry," Bloor said. "I don't know what got into me. I was just testing his sense of humor. He doesn't seem to have one."

"Bullshit. You were doing what you always do, being a deliberate jerk, and playing one of your little games. Tell me, John. Did you win that one, or not?"

He sat beside her and cracked his knuckles and stared at his hands. "To be honest," he said, looking up at her, noticing a golden teardrop earring, "I don't know how to keep you happy anymore. I felt like he was making fun of me."

"Oh, come on. He was being friendly. That's all."

"Friendly to you, yes."

Her glance was slanted, at least once removed from the room. "You're getting on better with Hammer, I see. I'm pleased about that. Let's settle for that for the time being." She stared at him for what seemed like a full minute. Bloor could hear the clock ticking. "I've talked to him about attending a traditional school. He's willing to give it a try, especially since the alternatives up here are limited."

"Goddamn it, we both agreed to come here, didn't we? Now you bring it up and throw it in my face?"

"Who's throwing anything in your face?" Phoebe pursed her lips and shook her head in exasperation, then her mouth tilted down, as though she might cry. "I don't understand the first thing about your moods, and you sure as hell don't seem to know much about mine. I get all dressed up for you, even put champagne on ice, and then you insult the next-door neighbor and screw everything up."

Bloor stared into the aquarium, then turned to her. "What do you see in me, anyway?"

Phoebe thought about his question. "There's a lot to see in you, John." She murmured something softly to herself, as though escaping from the tension of the moment into a song instead of a smoke. "There's also a lot to put up with. I just wish you could let go sometimes and admit how much you don't know. You take care of me, but you never ask for help, really. I don't think I've ever heard you ask for help." Her head twitched. An acute angle of sunlight broke into fiery blossom in her hair. "Look, I'm sorry, too.

Maybe I overreacted. I'm never happy for long. It's part of my nature. I told you that when you met me."

- - - - -

West, the neighbor, was a residential designer who worked at home. He began to take coffee with Phoebe. Bloor would sometimes drive up and find them huddled at the table, the curling steam of the coffee between them.

"Did you know Ron designed our house?" Phoebe asked. She was wearing a white turtleneck with blue dots and Bloor imagined that each dot was a fish. He wanted to tell his wife that she was living this afternoon in a world full of fish, but it was a flirtatious thing to say and Bloor did not want to say it in front of the architect. He wanted to take his wife to the aquarium and make love to her in its glow. It would be a small reconciliation and put to rest the recent tension between them, but it couldn't happen because the damned architect was in his house.

"Is that so?" he said, facing West, a childless widower. "Is that why I can never find clean towels?" He smiled, his muscles opening into the habitual lines that served him so well where he worked. "No, just kidding, Ron. How long have you been at it?"

"Years now, John. I like to work at home." He told Bloor about Reality Meditation. "After I lost my wife, I was devastated, as you might imagine. It was a form of therapy someone from the Baha'i House of Worship taught me. Don't think. Open yourself to the world. Watch the lotus blossom, or the angels on the head of a pin, or the fish in your aquarium. Whatever. Whatever turns you on. Let the good things settle. Let the junk float to the surface and wash away."

"Look, leave the aquarium out of it," Bloor said. "Any junk in that aquarium is supposed to be there." It was a sore spot, because in fact the water in the tank didn't look right, it was sort of muddy, a little cloudy all the time, and Bloor had taken to brooding about the fish, constantly checking water temperature and studying the ultraviolet sterilizer. "No offense meant," he added, glancing at Phoebe.

"None taken, John," West said. He studied Bloor over the rim of his tilted cup. "We have a group. Come join us sometime and see what you think."

Bloor put out his hands, one wrist crossed over the other, as though he expected to be tied up. "Have mercy," he said. "Anything but that."

- - - - -

One of the dwarfs died that year, and after a time the pygmy angel seldom ventured away from the stone Buddha. It would hover under one elbow, now thickly covered with algae.

Bloor continued to drive Hammer to school. "It's the *size* of the tank, Dad," Hammer argued earnestly in the spring, and produced from memory some statistics he had scared up while visiting the Shedd Aquarium.

"I respect that opinion, but to my mind the tank is plenty large, the mini-reef system provides lots of hiding places and lots of algae, and the sterilizer controls bacterial troublemakers." A tiny foreign car cut him off. It took a small act of will, but he refrained from leaning on the horn in deference to his stepson. "No, it's not the tank, or maintenance, and it's certainly not neglect. There's some unseen stress somewhere in the system."

At a red light Hammer pointed across a wide expanse of lawn. "Ron designed that place. It has mandalas in the floor, a spiral jetty instead of a back porch, and a gazebo wrapped in plastic."

"A spiral jetty," Bloor said.

"Dad, what about salt content?" Hammer adjusted the straps on his backpack, preparing to disembark as his father pulled to the curb. "Have you been monitoring that?"

Bloor snapped his fingers. "You may have hit it. It's always something obvious we forget, isn't it? Something we should have known all along. I'll go back home and check it out." He touched his stepson on the arm. "Hammer, you're forgetting your glove."

"Freudian slip." Hammer smiled shyly. "Don't expect too much, I'm no ballplayer. It's just a gym class."

- – – – –

The salt content was okay, but a night-blooming cereus next to the tank looked on its last legs. Bloor moved it to the other side of the room and stood for a minute by the drawn drapes, taking in the musty silence. The house seemed unusually quiet, and Bloor, feeling the onset of an anxiety attack, was tempted to kneel before the tank and scratch against its glass. Instead, he went looking for Phoebe in the bedroom. She wasn't there, and his anxiety increased, but he found her in the kitchen and his panic subsided a little. Her hair disheveled, still in her flannel robe, she was scrubbing the sink. "That's work you should save for the maid."

She jumped. "John! You scared the jesus out of me."

"You vacuum, dust, do the laundry. Leave it. Go to one of your personal growth seminars. Write in your journal."

"That's very tactful, John." She rubbed her forehead. "Look, I know we're supposed to have drinks at the Bernards', but I think I'm going to pass. Ron's group is meeting tonight." She offered Bloor an aggravated tight smile, an exasperated tilt of her hands. "If I go just to please you, we're on our way to a divorce."

"A divorce?" Bloor said, genuinely surprised. "Where the hell did that come from? Women." He tilted his head comically toward the heavens and grinned, but Phoebe was having none of it. She was staring at him. She sighed audibly. "Listen," Bloor continued, his voice earnest now, "I want to make you happy. That's my first priority." He paused and cracked his knuckles because he knew it irritated her. "But if we ever do split up, I want Hammer."

"What do you mean, you 'want' him? He's not even your kid."

"He is indeed my son."

"Get real, John."

"Get real?" Bloor nodded emphatically, then turned to the white wall and stood there, arms folded, jaw working, chin pointed a little up. "Do you mind if I ask you a question? Are you diddling with West?"

"Diddling?" She dropped a wire brush into the sink, where it glanced with a dull click against the drain. "Suppose Ron was a woman? Would you complain about two women who drank coffee together?"

"Maybe so. Damn right I would." Still facing the wall, Bloor considered the question more seriously. "It's not the same," he finally said.

"Why not?" She raised her hands in capitulation. "Never mind. Of course you're right. Have you ever been wrong?" She started chewing on a fingernail. "If home is where the heart is, maybe I don't have a heart anymore." She paused. "Or maybe we don't have a home, John."

Bloor turned from the wall. "Let's connect."

"I tell you what, John. You do what you have to do, I'll do what I have to do. When the two things connect, then we'll do something together. You think that might happen anytime soon, John? Because there's something in you which is hiding from me and won't come out. Do you think you might ever let me see it, whatever it is?"

"Let's go look at the fish," Bloor said. "We can talk there."

She stared at him so intensely that he decided to study the baseboard. "I feel sick," she said. "I feel like I have a fever."

Bloor felt far away from shore, on the lake, on water skis no longer attached to his feet. He went to the party alone that night, flirted outrageously, and woke long before dawn with night sweats, half-drunk, after dreaming of a woman just beyond his reach. He stared wildly around the curtained room, drowning for long seconds in amnesia.

When he realized Phoebe wasn't home yet, he looked in on Hammer, who was asleep, a copy of *Zen Mind, Beginner's Mind* propped open on the bed. Wind chimes, thin copper wafers tied together with fishing line, harmonized like a host of tiny voices in the steady rush of air from an air-conditioning vent. Bloor poured himself a drink and stared at the fish tank. The coral was still shining, breathing the water, and the open-sea clown fish, a pomacentrid that seemed never to sleep, was darting from shining coral, its usual habitat, to algae-green Buddha.

The pygmy angel was motionless, belly-up. It was floating transfigured in the aquarium's bright surface glare, as though it had spent the last of its material being in the presence of Buddha and spiritual truth.

Bloor had a tingling in his ankle, in his left wrist, a ringing in his ears. He measured his pulse and took a few deep breaths. Each time he looked at the fish, it was still dead. There was something about mixing invertebrates with angels in a single tank that he had to think about. There was something inhospitable in the aquarium, some mystery that had to be fathomed before he could sleep. But he was still too drunk and fatigued to think straight, so finally he fished out the dead pygmy with a small net and took it to the toilet.

For just a moment, getting giddy, he thought of swallowing the angel.

The impulse passed, however, and he flushed the fish without a benediction, then doused his face in the sink for a long time. The sound of water splashing on porcelain was reassuring, but his lids were heavy like lead sinkers and he felt a bit stupefied. He wanted to suspend the laws of chemistry and shrink himself to the size of an angel so that he could fit under Buddha's elbow.

At the aquarium, Hammer was sitting in the lotus position as close to the tank as he could reasonably get. His breathing was very deep, as though he was still asleep. When he turned with bright eyes and motioned silently, Bloor knelt on the geometrical parquetry and lowered his head. His breathing was labored and ragged. His nose whistled and his rotund belly hung over the waistband of his boxer shorts.

The floor was a dizzy patchwork, he now saw, some sort of mandala.

Bloor cupped his hands together. The boy, his eyes closed, hummed under his breath. It sounded like a double bass.

"Have mercy on me," Bloor said, closing his own eyes. He dredged up the words from some thirty years ago, finding the Jesus Prayer again as if emerging from a bout of amnesia. The prayer in those language days had been his daily penance. He raised his head self-consciously to see if Hammer was paying attention to him as he prayed. The boy's eyes were still closed, his face filled with artificial light and a deep humming sound still emerging preternaturally from someplace inside him.

"Have mercy on me," Bloor said. "Lord, have mercy. Have mercy on me." He repeated the words over and over, as if his life depended upon them, as if he was still uncertain about who he was and what his place in the world might be. In a trance, his head buzzing, he continued to pray, his eyes open. He stared into the aquarium. The clown fish was taking over the territory vacated when the angel went belly-up. Apparently contented with its new fate, it was nibbling at Buddha's algae-covered eyes, but the butterfly, hungry-looking, was swimming in ever-smaller circles, moving in for the kill.

BLACK ASH PINWHEEL

Once there was a perfect summer of love. I was Diane Keaton in a floppy hat, Clancy was the tiny daughter who could play with kitchen pots and pans as I cooked or snorted cocaine on the sly, and Jack, my husband, could sweep me off my feet every night and fuck me like nobody else could while I secretly dreamed of my fix.

Life was simple—love and peace and my next fix.

Here in California, halfway across the world from where I lived in that perfect time, before three judges issued bench warrants for my arrest, we have a graveyard for planes. Thousands squat here, the metal too fatigued for safety, placed in lost squadron formation. When Jack slings Clancy in my direction on a plane, I always fear the proximity of that graveyard. I've been afraid to fly for years, ever since rehab. When I was high, I would do anything: hot air balloon, paraglide, you name it. Now, on a few professional occasions, I've sweated the thing out, but mostly I arrange my schedule so that I can drive. Clancy's flight, with connections and layovers, takes five hours even in the best weather, and I'm scared to death when she's in the air. I know my fear is a delusion, but knowing doesn't help.

When she's somewhere above America, as she is now, on her way here for a long weekend, the only thing that comforts me is Black Ash Pinwheel. I keep it on my office desk. I'm a pencil-biter anyway, but on those days when she flies alone, I would chew the erasers off pencils if I didn't have Black Ash Pinwheel. It's a gift from Clancy—part robot, part pinwheel, and part bagpipe player. The size of a Raggedy Ann doll, it has a voice somewhere between the sound a pane of glass makes when rain strikes against it and the high faraway twang of a jetliner. When Clancy is in the air, I send it on desktop errands. The light on its head blinks, its drive mechanism hums like an old electric typewriter, it plays its quaint bagpipe ditty, and I'm content with its machined precision and metallic gleam, its every bolt riveted into place. If it works flawlessly, I reason, so will a jet plane. Its electric eye can sense and avoid solid objects, whether a piece of quartz with *Happy Birthday* calligraphed across it, a jagged piece of obsidian, or thick tomes of regulations. But it has no way to know when space runs out. I panic when it miscalculates and lurches like a drunk to the floor. If I fail to keep it safe, I imagine Clancy in her plane—toppling end over end, erupting into flame. "Clancy! Clancy!" I shout, rushing to the horrible scene, one cobbled together from newspaper accounts and disaster movies I hate but can't stay away from.

At the airport, dressed in a lacy cotton blouse and denim, waiting, not seeing me yet, she taps a foot and balances a magazine on her knees. Fidgeting, hat in hand, I greet her stiffly. "Hello, Clancy." When I gather her in, holding her frail body against mine, she abides me and offers her hand. "Hi, Mom. I'm glad to see you've survived the quake." She laughs the knowing laugh of a high school junior. "Won't get in a plane, but lives where the ground might fall out from under her."

"A small quake, barely made the news." I'm so nervous about saying the wrong thing, I almost go into my aspen act. I feel the blood rush to my head. "By our standards, not so bad. But the freeways are closed for repairs in places, so traffic is terrible." By the time I locate my car in the lot, she's telling me about the flight.

I keep an apartment large enough to accommodate a daughter accustomed to space, so my place echoes most of the year. The extra room is sparsely furnished, everything white. Standing in the doorway, she curtsies and touches me on the wrist. She looks me over. "That hat's still perfect. You look more like Diane every day." She fancies I look like Diane Keaton, an actress she favors because we saw her together, in *Annie Hall*, before I went AWOL. "When we were still a nuclear family," she likes to say, pausing significantly after "nuclear." She became entranced with the old dusty hat that Keaton wore even in the desert, according to the tabloids, and insisted I buy one like it. She was certain it would improve my image, especially if I wore it at a rakish angle, but it didn't keep me close to home, and I only dust it off now when she visits. It's one way to negotiate passage through those dreadful hours when we get to know each other all over again.

"Won't you join me for tea?"

She purses her lips and nods. "Sure, why not? It's one of those rituals that make you feel good, right? But it sure as hell feels quaint, don't it?" That's not quite the reply our game calls for, but I smile and prepare the hand-painted cups and saucers, the teaspoons and creamer and sugar bowl. She studies the bookshelves, the glass coffee table, the stack of unread magazines thrown helter-skelter on the floor, the trophy shelf above the television filled with odd neon sculptures in the shape of imaginary animals. "My Mommy-O," she says, "still a packrat." She presents a smile I've never seen before, almost looking over my shoulder, then letting her eyes travel down to my shoes and back again. It frightens me. I'm dowdy and dumb, I think, though I know it isn't true. My life is in order, my wardrobe up to snuff. One day at a time, I tell myself. That story. We sit on the couch, courteous, but I don't know what to do about the new kind of tension. I find my fingers in my mouth and sit on them. I catch myself biting my lower lip. I make talk as small as rain and feel the two of us slipping into our own daydreams. Then the room shakes, the teacups rattle in their saucers, and a neon tube falls flat on the shelf.

I've never talked with her about my breakdown—the booze, the drug-addled decision to run off with a drug-addled man, the compulsion to find rock bottom, those bench warrants, the credit cards I filched and used, the long rehab, the relapse, the other rehab that took. That story. My husband found himself someone more stable, made his move when the making was good, and took custody. It was fair enough—I lived in my car for a time, traded sex for dope. That story. But I got back my pride and my life years ago, I go to twelve-step almost every day, take my meds at the appointed hours.

"Aftershock," I say. "Very mild. Nothing to worry about."

"Wow! Like rock and roll, huh?" She puts out her arms and pretends to fight for balance. "That was neat. Can you do it again?"

"What? I didn't do it. It's not my place that's moving, it's the ground."

"Hey, lighten up. I'm teasing." She smiles graciously, like a woman twice her age.

"Of course," I say, nonplussed. I tidy up the neon and we drink tea. "I have a few things to pick up at the office," I hear myself say, though it's only technically true—the things could wait. I can't sit still, though, my body feels like it's going to take me to the balcony of my place and throw me over the rail into the pool. "Why don't you come along?" On the way out, she does a kind of old-fashioned waltz and curtsies, getting me to laugh. She knows how her flight affects me. It's as though she disappears halfway between her father and me, lost in some sort of national daydream. I'm afraid she might disappear the way I once did. I imagine disasters, abductions, and kidnappings. A terrorist planting a bomb on the plane. Once, in a panic before a flight, I called her and told her to skip it, that the "vibes" weren't right. She giggled. "Oh, this is too much. Now I know you're California." She called my ex-husband to the phone and they had a laugh together. "No! She didn't say that. Did she? Really?" He came on the phone. "Did you really say that?"

There's a lot of finger tapping in the car.

"Are you glad to be here?" I ask, swerving into the right-hand lane.

"Who wouldn't be glad? Three whole days in California. What could be better?" she says. She reaches over and touches my hair, another new gesture. She stares straight ahead through the windshield. Thousands of cars are crawling east, but we're going west. "So like this is California."

I stare blankly.

"Going, going, gone," she laughs, pointing to her forehead and staring significantly at me. I have blankouts, I call them, a kind of dry drunk some days, and I come to myself in a panic, not sure if I fell off the wagon. Maybe I'm having one now; I live in a place where at night coyotes howl for the blood of my neighbor's pet dog and the desert wind makes the mountains sound haunted. Some nights I hear the coyotes in my head and the wind just outside my door, as though I should tug on the floppy hat and head for the high country.

Time passes in the car but I'm not aware of it, off somewhere beyond words. I drift into a final cloverleaf and leave the freeway to avoid some construction, but end up a little lost, negotiating my way through a bad neighborhood. "Mad psycho killer time."

"Mad psycho killers?" she says. "Maybe California isn't really like, you know, the best place to spend the summer."

"I thought the summer was a done deal," I say. "I've been making plans for us." It's clear she has an agenda, but before she can advance it she notices a car approaching us in the dark without its headlights. "Flick your brights, tell that guy to put his lights on."

"No way. Gangs cruise around like that. It's an initiation rite. To get in the gang, you got to kill somebody. You got to kill the first driver who flicks his brights at you."

"Bullshit."

"Clancy," I say. "Is that how we brought you up? I can't believe you talk like that."

"You didn't bring me up at all."

The car gets quiet again. "I'm sorry," she says. "I didn't mean it like that."

"Yes, you did," I say. "And it's all right. And it's true."

"But not to change the subject," she says. "I still can't believe you really think that guy might kill you if you flick your brights at him. That's crazy."

"Still crazy. That's me. And still alive."

"So, like, I guess you believe in the vanishing Elvis, too, right?"

"Elvis can go wherever he wants. Just so long as you don't disappear."

It was the wrong thing to say. I have no idea what to say. I say the first thing that pops into my egg-fried brain. Pieces lost long ago, memories lost or patched over with hallucinations. I trip, if you know what I mean.

In the office, she does another little dance near my desk and bows to Black Ash Pinwheel. She sits in my chair and flicks the switch on and off, giggling at the squeaky bagpipe music.

"You know," she says, "that sound did it. There were so many other things I could have bought for someone of your, um, advanced age"—she laughs—"but that music could not be denied." Black Ash Pinwheel performs its tricks like a dog fresh from obedience school. Sensing the obsidian paperweight, a mountain rising from the piedmont, it makes a smart military turn. To negotiate the descent from an ink blotter to the wooden desktop, it pivots on its base. Two lights on its forehead blink out my name in Morse code. It bows mechanically and makes more music.

"Neat, huh?" She props her chin on the book of regulations. As Black Ash Pinwheel swivels, buzzes, totters, and backtracks, her fingers mimic its movements, and I remember how she learned about the world by doing everything we did exactly the way we did it. "There's no going back, is there?" I hear myself say.

She stares at me, that sliding glance again. "The thing is, we have to talk about this summer. It's getting weird, you know, disappearing from my life for a summer? I mean, not that I don't want us to get close. And the thing is, we are close, way close, and Dad, he doesn't worry anymore, the way he did, he trusts you too, but I have this chance, you know, to go to Europe."

"Oh." My stomach turns. "That's great, Clancy."

"Yeah. Dad might come along as, you know, a chaperon? You guys can talk about it." She touches a finger to one drawn-in cheek and frowns. "Of course, you know, I could live out here when I go to college. I mean, not with you, but in this area? That's, like, something to think about. You know?"

I don't say anything, but I turn to the window and stare out at the city and think how everybody's somebody else and nobody lives anywhere. Jack is a kind man, but I won't push my luck with him. I fucked up long ago and forgiveness is only one thing in a long line; if he wants to go with Clancy to Europe, I have no brief to fight. There was a time during rehab when suicide made the most sense—so much lost, so many years gone, nothing the same. Why keep on keeping on without the kick of booze and drugs? I did keep on, though, found self-respect, and the moment passed, but there have been other moments since then, and I think now that such moments are meant to remind me of something.

Now and then when I pick up my ringing phone there's nobody on the line, and I wonder whether Jack tried to reach me from the time of that perfect summer of love, before he knew that anything was wrong, before I knew that anything was really wrong. I imagine a gate or a door, a time warp back to those days. I dream of starting over. Then I realize that there is no such thing as starting over, at least not with the same people. And after a while, nobody on the line and the bedside clock gleaming out its numbers, I make a cup of tea and sit on the balcony outside my apartment and stare into the placid blue waters of the swimming pool, so perfect and so blue.

Clancy, a little flustered—mission accomplished—turns back to Black Ash Pinwheel. Outside, a plane descending flies past the window, its landing lights superimposed on Black Ash Pinwheel's blinking movements. Black Ash Pinwheel falls from the desk—nothing so d to veer away from—and tumbles to the carpet. It keeps pumping out its bagpipe dirge. It is a dirge, I realize, not the anthem that I imagined. Clancy, reflected pale in the window, still intensely involved with Black Ash Pinwheel, picks it up and checks it for damage. It moves again—proudly, I think—and she urges it on.

"Black Ash Pinwheel," I whisper. "That summer. That hat. That story." Black Ash Pinwheel, like a pet, is the object that serves as our go-between, but like the plane that flies her cross-country, it can bring her so close and no closer. I'm not sure whether Clancy hears me or not, but for a dizzy moment, rapping out the syllables of the past, of an imaginary time and place when all of us lived together in a perfect summer of love, I rise above myself, ready to fly, able to go anywhere.

SPENDING THE DAY

WITH DONALD TRUMP

All the way to her address I see dead dogs by the road. The papers say somebody from somewhere, probably addicted, has thrown the poisoned animals up and down the tree-lined avenue, at the entranceway to an acre and a half of house, in front of a bank or church, behind the rear wheel of a Rolls. Whether it means anything or not is the ten-thousand-dollar question. That's the reward. In this neighborhood a pedigreed dog gets a burial and a tombstone. At her address they put flowers on the graves of dogs.

The local cops are shaking the ivy, after the culprit. I pull past the mansion, nestled in a circle of trees a long way from the street, and park in the drive. Without knocking, I enter, my briefcase of tools in one hand. "Man in the hallway! Man in the hallway!" I shout, climbing the stairs. The bathroom door at the end of the hallway is closed, I imagine lace panties. "Typewriter man!" I scream, taking no chances. At her door, I rap like Woody Woodpecker.

She opens it, rubbing Irish eyes until they're full of freckles. She thinks she can hear me, see me full way round, only I'm looking at myself through her eyes, the way I'm bunched up inside my pants, the way my eyes go glassy and distant when I'm aroused, the way I reach for myself. At dinner, she'll tell them, all those people who come here every few weeks and talk as food is placed before them, that I'm only twenty years out of date. She'll call me eccentric, guess about my toupee. But she won't tell them what my head looks like without the hair. She won't tell them what I keep in my pockets.

"I've developed a relationship with this typewriter," she says, motioning me to her cubbyhole. "If you can fix it, whack it and get

it going, I'd certainly show my appreciation." It's an unhealthy relationship, I think about saying, but I smile brightly. "Trouble is,"
she continues, "it won't go. In Ireland, we don't have electric typewriters."

"Or computers?" I add.

She pauses and hears what she's saying. I'm getting ideas about
an overseas franchise. "At least I don't. So when this one doesn't
go, you see, I think it's me. But it's not. It's plugged in, you see, it's
turned on, it hums, but it won't go. It's defective."

"Let me have a look, lassie," I say in my best brogue. "Sometimes a good whack in the potato is all a thing needs, you're right
about that, but the world is more technical than you think. You
never know what might come crawling through your window."
She'll imitate that brogue over coffee in the breakfast room, only
she can't describe how flea powder replaces talc, the way it tickles
the nose. I tinker here, tinker there, caressing the machine, keeping up the chatter. *Now is the time for all good men to come to the aid
of their party*, I type. The *y* leaps off the page.

"It's not stuck, you see," she says. "When it works, it doesn't
quite."

"Yes. Believe me, lassie, I know typewriters. This needs the
shop. We'll get you a computer instead."

"No," she said. "I never compute."

I laughed politely. They come from anywhere, by invitation, to
the mansion, deeded for the good of literature in a dead man's will.
I knew that dead man before he was dead. I expected he would
leave a little something to me because I did him favors, brought
him all sorts of treats he couldn't get anywhere else. He lived alone
except for the help, but often enough his city friends stayed somewhere on the premises. When he took sick and died, what he left
me was trade.

When I first brought the Irish one her typewriter, a Swikswatch,
sleek and Oriental, I gave her a wink. "What do you people really
do here?" I said. She would retell that one, too, but after my question her eyes fluttered. She was stuck for a smart reply. There was

no lock on her door, I noticed, no chain. Outside her vine-covered window the roof sloped like a woolly mammoth almost to the garden, where there were benches and chairs. I knew after dark there were no garden lights. "You from Ireland?" I asked, letting her off the hook.

"Yes, Kilkenny," she said, absolutely polite, suddenly a bit frightened. I was the real thing, you see. I was what everyone talked about over there, a real American man, real enough to take her breath away.

"Yeah? You must be really glad to get away from all those bombs."

All the way back to my shop I could imagine her storing that one away. "Ireland to his mind is this little lay-by where everyone's ducking bombs." People should take advantage of what they have. Sure enough, I thought, locking the shop and preparing my solution—bane of dog, hair of woman, gland of frog. And then the assorted drugs. I know enough about drugs to be a pharmacist.

But some people have too much. I drive down these streets, see houses big enough for half of Oakland to live in. They're hidden behind clipped hedges, behind a Sherwood Forest of trees, all protected by elaborate security and Dobermans, all manicured by truckloads of maintenance men, little Mexicans who get peanuts, all patted down by interior designers, cooks, servants, dog shrinks. I know these people think they can do whatever they want. All those rooms, all those closed doors.

You live in a duplex without a yard, everybody knows your business, when your old man comes home drunk, when he takes out the strap. You live in a castle, people imagine Palm Beach, Beverly Hills, even in a geriatric ward like this, where people turn thirty and look smug, like their lives are over. I got screwed up before I could come into my own, I'm not so crazy I don't know that. What I had, got lost. The Irish lass, she has a sense of humor, what she takes advantage of gives pleasure. We're much alike, she and I. We deserve a night together.

But take Donald Trump. He has friends down the street. I read about him in the papers, all that property, that money. Stretch limos, a big yacht, cellular phones everywhere. He has his troubles now, woman troubles, money troubles, maybe a dead dog at his gate, but I studied the man when he owned that New Jersey football team.

"What you writing, lassie, a play?" I ask, hefting the replacement, an old faithful Selectric, into the cubbyhole beside the shelf: tin can of ink pens, stack of bonded paper, note cards with illegible scribble, Tylenol, vitamin pills, alarm clock, books.

"You must be a prognosticator," she says. "You're exactly right."

She's flirting, and I tease from her when she goes to sleep, what kind of schedule the house keeps.

"Let me guess," I say in my brogue. "It's a play about women and firecrackers and the Fourth of July, three things that go together like Mom, the flag, and apple pie."

She smiles brightly. I've overdone it, she walks clear round me, sees me from several sides. I almost give it away. "Well, it's a voice play," she finally says. "It's not exactly about anything. Oh, that's not right. Maybe it's about the things we lose. It's sort of performance art. You know, Philip Glass, David Byrne, Robert Wilson? *Koyaanisqatsi, The Knee Plays, The Catherine Wheel?* You try to hear a voice to get it down, then the interplay of voices, then a kind of sound track."

I shrug. "People should take advantage of what they have. Performance art, that's like the dead dogs around the village, right? I mean, photograph them, write about them, maybe get a statement from the culprit for the museum wall, do a mug shot. Maybe look at his diary or his altar."

"That's a little extreme, wouldn't you say so?" she asks uneasily.

At least she's heard about the dogs. "Like the Irish bombs, then?"

"Okay, then, like the bombs if you insist."

"You want to hear voices," I say. "You ought to do like that woman. She speaks for some guy, Ramses or something, who's thirty-five thousand years old. He lives on a mountain in Tibet.

She gets into a trance and comes on in a deep voice, very seductive. She makes a mint. Hauls them in with a hook, all the yo-yos."

"Yes, well, each to her own," she says primly. "We have to give a voice, or a face, to what we want." She studies my face for a long time. "You seem to know a lot about it."

"I keep my eyes open. I pay attention." I can see I'm wearing out my welcome. "But you're right. It all comes out in the wash. Try the thing out," I say, pointing. "If it's not to your liking, I'll bring you a computer for the same price. Introduce you to the new millennium, American style."

She pecks at it. There's a porcelain knob beneath a mirror nailed above her small bureau. On the knob she's hung some jewelry: a pearl necklace, a turquoise bracelet.

I'm edging from the room now, my hand deep in one pocket. She's only hearing me with one ear; she's already developing a relationship with the Selectric. "I'd give Donald Trump my dough, but on one condition only. I don't have to *see* the man, I don't have to *talk* to the man, and I don't have to *think about* the man. Let the man do his thing, but keep him off the grass. "

"Trump?" she says absentmindedly.

The next morning there's a dead dog on the front stoop.

I can see how it plays. She stares at the typewriter. During the night somebody touched her, there was something in her mouth. She may have been dreaming; she may have been drugged. She can't quite remember, her blood is heavy. Some jewelry seems to be misplaced, but maybe she left it back home. There's a kind of suction feel to her pucker, no taste when she eats toast. She's not sure who to tell what to. She sits in the kitchen for hours with cold coffee, willing to listen to anything, anyone, waiting for voices, faces, for stories or even rumors, marking time until the dinner bell. She blames it on her new typewriter.

WOMEN OF THE BROWN ROBES

Elaine stood on the steps of the Unitarian Church waiting for Patsy, her best friend, but it was Oscar who appeared first at her side. He tried to give her all the money in his wallet.

She stared at him. "Is this a payoff or what?" She shaded her eyes from the bright sun. In the temple basement, a fellowship service was about to begin, but hours earlier Oscar had done his damnedest to get those long delicate fingers of his under her silk blouse. For years, his fingers had guided Elaine from chopsticks through the various moods of a sonata, but last night he had tried to play a different kind of music on parts of her body that had nothing to do with the piano.

She had been stunned. He was tall and sallow, granted, but quite charming in his old-fashioned way, like an Ichabod Crane kissed by the pope. There was always a vase of flowers near his piano, and next to it a tray with a pitcher of hot tea, cubes of sugar, and wedges of lemon. A metronome made of mahogany that stood like a pagan sentinel next to the flowers was as heavy as a stone paperweight. "If this is a payoff, Oscar, forget it. The whole thing, I mean, the lessons, the drinks, everything."

"You don't understand," he whispered, glancing at the empty schoolyard on one side of the temple and a parking lot on the other. "I depend for my livelihood on word of mouth. One indiscretion, Elaine, especially in this Peyton Place, and I am doomed, absolutely doomed." He adjusted his cravat and shrugged to settle the coat around his waist.

Elaine had faith that a good day was a better drug than the anti-depressant she sometimes took, and today flowers were bright like decals, the wind was high, and the heavens had the speckled texture of a robin's egg. If she were in Alaska, she thought, she would be standing watch with the Women of the Brown Robes. "Listen to your voice," they would be saying. All of them had given up families, careers, and fortunes. Elaine much preferred their imagined company to that of people. She turned from Oscar, shaded her eyes, and squinted, trying to get back to Alaska and those calm voices so hard lately to find inside her head. A bunch of kids across the street were playing one-two-three red light in the front yard of a yellow house. A towheaded youngster, still in his Sunday suit, was "it." Each time he turned, stranded on the sidewalk, the other kids crept closer. He moved fast, but one girl was faster. The boy untucked his shirt, tossed away his tie, even cheated by twisting his neck before shouting the words, but she always stopped a step or two closer with a trickster smile as bright as sunlight on the azaleas.

Elaine was still in love with Kevin, her ex-husband, even though he had moved across the country to California and had fallen in with a cult. She had thought she knew him down to the marrow in his bones, but the voice inside his head these days was one she no longer recognized. His phone calls were about audits and bad thoughts and sweating inside a sauna at the center, but she could remember a time before they became high school sweethearts, when promise was everything. On a trampoline in the gym, he had performed double flips and back flips, defying the laws of gravity for her while she leaned against the waxy folded bleachers, pretending to be indifferent. On their first date, they had drunk Coca-Cola and danced in swirling light in the same gym, one bedecked for the occasion with ribbons and crepe paper that gave the illusion of glamour. Quaint, chivalric, he had docked her at her door after the chaperoned evening while his father waited in the car, eyes averted. He had placed his hands stiffly on her shoulders, probably following the old man's directions. He was a head taller than she was, at that unwieldy age some people take years to suffer through.

He rubbed his lips against hers, her first kiss, but she flew away from him, her mind on the trampolines that had been all folded up for the evening along the gym walls behind crepe paper and tinsel. When he had turned away, red-faced, his father tapping the horn, she had been relieved, and had jumped high enough to touch the ceiling tiles inside the front entrance.

"You've got to promise you won't quit taking lessons," Oscar said. "I mean, I'm willing to compensate you for any lessons you feel you took under false pretenses. That's fair, isn't it?"

"A bribe, Oscar?" His shirt was never untucked, his cuff links never undone. Not a single greased strand of thinning hair was ever out of place. He chose his cologne, he once told her, because it had the fragrance of his first piano. "Look," she said, "you made a pass. Big deal." She clicked her tongue. "This is a hard time for me, Oscar. I thought I could depend on you. Instead you pawed me and told me I've been your mental wife for months. What was that supposed to mean?"

"I just drank too much wine," he whispered. "I have a drinking problem. I'm not supposed to drink, it does something to my metabolism. I get crazy." He nodded at several parishioners, who returned his greeting and disappeared into the temple. "You held my hand, didn't you?" he said, his blue eyes going gray. "You don't call that leading me on?"

He turned on his heels and followed the others.

Patsy arrived in a floppy hat the color of tree bark, a loose-brimmed hat two generations old that shimmied in the sunlight, a garage-sale hat. Patsy called it her traveling hat, and used it mostly on days her job as a caseworker required house calls. She swept Elaine into the basement, a low-ceilinged room as long as a small gym. The minister, a wiry marathon runner, put them in a circle and opened his arms, as though to enclose everyone in his benevolence. "Let's greet each other with a smile, followed by a handclasp of fellowship," he said. Everyone dutifully followed his instructions. "Good. Now, let's imagine we're in the woods. There's a great waterfall above us." He rocked his hands to simulate ripples.

"Can you hear it, cascading down, blotting out anxiety, helping us relax, helping us witness our lives?"

Patsy tickled Elaine's palm, reminding her to hold hands. The real estate salesman on her right grabbed her fingers so fiercely he almost broke bones. Across the circle, Oscar alternated disdainful stares with beagle-like mooning. There was something odd about him today. He looked as if he had slept in his clothes. Elaine's hands started sweating, as they did whenever anybody wanted something from her. She was not much for fellowship services. Her stories were always outlandish, despite a sincere desire to change. She was always turning some soap opera or movie plot into autobiography. "A Mexican general flew into a mountainside when I left him," she would say in a deadpan voice. "Now, is that tragic or what?"

"I have something to say," Oscar announced, surprising even the minister, who had never quite figured him out. The service sometimes functioned as a forum on a current controversy, but more often someone broke into a crying jag. Everyone would encircle the aggrieved party and the minister would serve up, as though in a chalice, some Emersonian proverb. Because Oscar had little patience with such things, most of the congregation found him repulsive, too much the aesthete, hunching his shoulders in a flinch whenever the language got too rough. But Elaine and Patsy were his students, familiar with the shoe-polish fragrance of his cologne. They valued his predictability. He was the only man they figured they could trust.

"Well, Oscar, let's have it," the minister said.

"Love is everything," Oscar said. He flinched a little and stared at the floor. "Without love, there would be nothing."

Everyone waited, but that was it. "Hey Oscar," Patsy whispered to Elaine, "how about some of the juicy details?" Elaine studied a piece of bubble gum so ground into the gray carpet that it looked like an old penny.

Everyone surrounded Oscar and lovebombed him, a few parishioners taking sadistic delight in Oscar's discomfort. Patsy told him she loved him in a voice that sounded sincere. She laid a hand on his butt and batted her eyelashes. Oscar grew as pink as the inside of a frankfurter until the group's attention turned to the real estate salesman. He launched into a diatribe about a lost sale, his anger filling the air like a virus.

"Elaine," the minister finally said, "you have anything this week?" It was her cue for comic relief; he wanted to wind things down.

"I just cannot stand all this light anymore," she said, gesturing broadly to make clear that she did not mean the fluorescent ceiling. "In Alaska, where the Women of the Brown Robes live, their voices are clean and cold. They take vows of poverty."

A few parishioners exchanged glances, but the minister did not mistake her tone. "Elaine, isn't that a little elaborate?"

"No," she said. "That was the message of Christ, to give everything up and follow his voice. Or am I mistaken?" She kept putting her hand on her cheek, as if to hide a birthmark.

"No, not exactly, Elaine, though some choose to do that."

"Well, I so choose. We all of us should so choose. Jesus had himself a clear, clean voice inside his head. Did he not? Alaska is not easy. Azaleas do not grow there. The sun sometimes does not come up at all. Just because the weather is great does not mean we should feel good about the world. When the Women kill an animal in Alaska, they apologize to it. Everything is alive. People, animals, trees. I don't want a lovebomb, I want to *do* something. Why is it that we do not go down to the wrong side of the tracks and listen? Don't any of you get tired of hearing the same voice inside your head each day?"

"Look, Elaine," the minister said, "I'm too tired to deal with this right now. If you're serious, we do need volunteers. For that matter, we have connections faraway. You could go with the Habitat people to San Diego and build houses." He rubbed his hands together. "I tell you what. Try not to sell your house before you come see me. We'll talk about it, but let's close for now with a meditation. All anger and fear must be forgotten before it can be surpassed."

Patsy gave Elaine a stricken look. What she liked, Elaine knew, was the tavern where they walked in the shade of maples and oaks to drink something sweet after the service. Usually, Oscar would tell them stories. He read, exclusively, the biographies and critical studies of great composers. The voices inside his head were very dependable. He would have the week's choicest anecdote rehearsed: how Cocteau, Satie, and Picasso collaborated with Diaghilev on a ballet, for instance.

Elaine was not in the mood. "Patsy, I'm lonely," she said when they hit the sidewalk. "I'm lonely all the time. The only people who keep me company are the Women."

"Is that a confession? Should I give you some shit for getting down on yourself or do you just need me to listen?" She was a short woman whose back had an S-curve in it and she trotted to keep up with Elaine.

"I miss Kevin. I wish we were together again."

"Is that possible? Does Kevin want In again or just you?"

Elaine shrugged. "I don't know. He hangs out with people who put little words in his head. He pays tons of money to take courses that any real religion would offer for free. But what do you expect? The sun is way too bright out there, and it *always* shines. Whenever I visit, I get migraines." She rubbed her forehead. "The sun isn't even working *here* the way it should. I'm ready for Alaska, Patsy, a different way of life."

"Then do it."

"You are exactly right. I should leave right now. Right this second. I would if I could."

"Shoulda, woulda, coulda," Patsy said, one of her refrains. "You stopped taking your meds, didn't you?"

"Don't play therapist with me," Elaine said.

"Elaine, have you ever been to Alaska? Even on a cruise, I mean? Even for a weekend?" She jogged along in her flats. She could listen to Elaine when Elaine was near tears without bringing them on, and Elaine knew it. Kevin would tighten up, his jaws working, and the minister lapse into his psychobabble, but Patsy let her go on, so she did. "This morning I wanted cigarettes. I started smoking unfiltered Lucky Strikes and quit with True. That was *years* ago, Patsy, but this morning I wanted a smoke. I was lonely for a cigarette, for what we used to do. We used to go to the park down the street. Smoke, drink, feed the ducks. There was a dinky playground, park benches, a slide. A few kids tossing a baseball."

Patsy shrugged. She took off her hat and twirled it on a finger. "You're in Waiting. If Kevin wants In, then Waiting is all right. Otherwise, you've got to work on Letting It Go."

"I guess then I'm lucky, right?" Elaine said. "You-all could have loved *me* to death back there instead of Oscar."

"Don't forget, Elaine, I'm a card-carrying member of a helping profession. Love bombs are good for the soul."

Elaine stopped before a rosebush to take home a flower as an act of rebellion but got herself stuck by a thorn. A drop of blood appeared on one thumb and grew to the size of a dime before she sucked on it. "That's it," she said. "With me and Kevin, there were never enough thorns. Too much friction, not enough thorns." She clutched Patsy's forearm. "Come to Alaska with me. It will be hard on you. You will find it testing your mettle."

Oscar overtook them. He had his tie in one hand. His neck was blotchy. He was gulping air. "Elaine, may I have a word?"

"Sure, Oscar."

Oscar glared at Patsy. She shrugged and waved them ahead. They crossed a street and walked into a small park with lanes and hedges. "Alaska?" Oscar shivered. "That's just like you, I guess, running off on a fling."

"Not a fling, Oscar. A pilgrimage, a soul adventure."

"I see." He paused. "But you held my hand, Elaine. When we held hands, I just assumed . . ." He trailed off, as though seeing the flaw in a grand Aristotelian design. "I know you like adventure. You told us about that Mexican general, that fling in Brazil with your Peace Corps friend."

Elaine bit her lip. "Look, Oscar, I make that stuff up. I do not mean to mislead you. Nobody else believes a thing I say."

He frowned. "And you said you wanted to take advantage of your freedom. You said that to me when we were alone, just the two of us. Did you make that up, too? What about those women you talk about all the time?" He gripped her arm fiercely. "Life isn't meant to be taken with a grain of salt," he said. "Salt is bad for the blood. You seduced me and you didn't even mean it. Don't you ever listen to yourself?" He pulled his arm away from her, as if she was the one holding on to him, and stalked off, his head bobbing above the shrubs.

Ah, holding hands, she thought, walking alone in the park. She could remember lying in bed and mooning all night after holding one of Kevin's hands most of the evening. She would scribble the magical name in her notebook, *Kevin Kevin Kevin.* She would place her name next to his—Kevin *Gould Elaine Gould Mrs. Gould*—say it a dozen times for the sound before destroying the page, entrusting to her diary only some cryptic word to mark the ritual: *EG, eleven letters, what if.* Hand-holding for beginners should be a required high school course, she thought. Your palms sweat, your fingers get stubby and stiff like pieces of chalk. Long before she married Kevin, years before the sun got too bright, she would try to figure out when to give him her hand or how long to let him hold it. Much later, the marriage winding down, they would tussle in bed, too full of aggravation for anything else. They would hand-wrestle and forget their latest fight, neither one hurting the other with an accidental-on-purpose slip of a fingernail or a grip too tight for fun; some invisible necklace of affection was still unbroken between them.

Standing on her back porch, she heard her phone ring. She fumbled with her keys and they fell with a clink, small slivers of bright metal. She thought about leaving them there on the stoop, along with the rest of her life, especially the glass that let in too much light. Alaska is cold, she thought, and I'm not used to privation, but there it is. She blushed when she thought of her makeup and perfume and earrings. The Women would take a look and laugh themselves sick.

It was Kevin on the phone. "I'm getting married," he said. "Did I tell you about her? I met her at the center. She's helping me get rid of all my bad thoughts." When they had lived together, she had yelled all the time, she remembered, screamed about everything, and the most he gave in return was a frown as thin as a Communion wafer.

She poured a glass of tea and garnished it with mint. What would the Women be drinking about now? Bitter laced with licorice, the snow swirling as they held hands and prayed between sips of hot tea. Pearls of moisture collected on her own glass. Ice cubes clinked. Ice, she thought. In Alaska, it connects everything. Water, snow, ice, frozen air. It connects land to water, water to air, air to land.

She consoled herself with such thoughts until dusk.

The following Sunday they talked about toxic waste. "I found out they're testing for PCBs in the courthouse where I work," said Frank Holliday, a heavyset man with a homegrown voice. Elaine, sitting next to him, could hear its timbre inside her head. "But what can I do? Quit? I have a family."

Patsy nodded. "Yeah, you all know they checked my office for asbestos? Some men with ladders and a little meter? They won't tell me zilch about the results. We need to get organized. The military used to spray our cities with poison, just to see how the stuff carried in the atmosphere. We need to get radical again. The sixties have to come back."

Across the circle, Oscar smiled like a sheet of shaken aluminum foil. "Why don't you shut your mouth, you stupid bitch."

"What?" Patsy said, leaning forward.

His shirt was soaked with sweat. "All I did was touch one of you, just touch you after you led me on, and what happens? I see you smirking. Satans, all of you! Every one."

There was stunned silence. When he left, his shoes echoed on the metal stairs like gunshots. Patsy surged after him in her floppy traveling hat, calling out his name.

The minister stepped forward. "Patsy is a professional," he said, holding out a hand like a traffic cop. "She'll help Oscar find the help he needs. Now, it's time to meditate. We've never had such need of it. Everyone, take a deep, calming breath. Please. Do it now. There's nothing to be afraid of, nothing to worry about. Breathe deeply." He cupped his hands behind his neck to demonstrate a way to breathe from the abdomen. "Let your thoughts move like the tides, like the ocean. Listen to my voice." He lowered his head until his bald spot gleamed in the light like a doorknob. "Close your eyes. Let your mind go wherever it will."

Elaine opened the door and stepped into Alaska.

"Good," the minister said. "Stay there, wherever you choose. Go deeper and relax, as I count to ten."

It was forty below, inky, silent except for the wind. When it stopped whistling, Elaine, with the Women, heard someone outside the cabin cock a rifle, a sound clear like a door snapping shut. She prayed for a quick, clean kill. "So many voices, so many people saying so many things," one of the Women said.

Four, he counted. "Good," he said. "Nowhere to go, nothing to do, not even a reason to ask why."

Five. They lived on prayer, their souls clean like new snow.

She heard Oscar and Patsy, their voices coming to her as if from a great distance.

Six. Seven. Eight.

She stretched her fingers, the same fingers that tried to play the preludes of Chopin. She longed to hold hands with the Women, but her fingers felt plump, sweaty, and incapable of grace. She leaned forward as far as she could, holding her stretch in every muscle and bone until the room echoed with footsteps. "Holy shit!" Frank Holliday shouted.

She opened her eyes and took in the scene. Frank Holliday was grimacing, one of his arms dangling uselessly at his side. Patsy sat against a wall. She was staring blankly around the room. The minister was sitting dazed on the floor, holding the side of his head and moaning.

Oscar, staring at Elaine, stood beside the minister. His blue eyes had gone gray. He had his mahogany metronome in one hand and his wallet in the other. "Elaine," he said, and squinted. "That is your name, isn't it?"

"Oscar."

"Elaine," he said. He hurled the metronome wildly in her general direction and it bounced on the carpet with dull thuds. He approached Elaine and raised his wallet over her head; he shook it like a hankie, showering her with dollar bills, credit cards, claim checks, and a single foil packet. When he was finished, the wallet empty, he dropped it and sat down at her feet. He stared up at her. His eyes were blue and placid again like an unruffled lake. His hands were in his lap and his mouth a little open, so that Elaine was dizzy looking down, as though seeing herself in his eyes and hearing for the first time the real voices of rage inside her head, voices as complicated as musical phrases ringing out one against another in a fugue.

BATTLE OF NEW ORLEANS

I cured a guy once of schizophrenia, against orders, using ketchup. Despite my official title as a psychological aide, I considered myself a method counselor, trying to turn metal into gold, floating into the heads of patients the way I floated through my tour of duty. "Just mind the store and keep Thompson in the dayroom so he don't have one of his fits," the chief social worker told me. She tied a pastel scarf around her neck. "I don't want him messing around." Arching a penciled-in eyebrow, she looked up at me from her wheelchair. "And I don't want to hear about no mischief from you, neither. You hear what I'm saying? I can't keep covering for you when you screw up."

"Yes, ma'am," I said, floating politely through my shift. The tone was one of my masks. She scowled, taking the remark for the put-down it was intended to be—one more reprimand and I was out the door. At that time in my life, every door revolved soon enough, occasionally for their reasons but mostly for my own.

She leaned toward me and gripped the wheels of her chair, but before the discussion had a chance to continue, her buddy the behaviorist hurried past in his fedora. She called out a greeting and trundled off with him to the van outside, the two of them discussing a new token system. The van was already packed with patients and staff going on a field trip to the old fort downriver for a reenactment of the Battle of New Orleans.

I had a sincere aversion to battles, so I was left on the ward with the incorrigibles. The on-duty nurse, complaining about her taxes, promptly wandered away into the administrative wing. Two of the incorrigibles screamed from time to time in their solitary padded cells.

Thompson was in the dayroom; he was wearing a hat with dog-ears and talking to a game show host. At the old fort, a cannon went off. "The Union must and shall be preserved," Thompson shouted to the leisure-suited slickster on the television that was bolted to the wall above his head. Thompson motioned to me with a grandiloquent wave. "Today I'm investigating everything there is to know about clay," he said. "I think about clay the way some people think about Christ." The right side of his face contracted spasmodically—trigeminal neuralgia, according to the chart. "Why don't you unlock the clay for me?"

"Sorry. We stay in the dayroom. Orders."

"Orders?" Thompson put his tobacco-stained fingertips to his lips and kissed me off, then jumped up in his surplus pajamas to stare through window mesh at a tangle of electrical wires and trans-formers across the yard. "Clay is a fine-grained substance used in bricks and pots. Clay everywhere, man. You just don't have eyes to see." He tapped his forehead against the mesh. "Living with clay is like, where you live going *everywhere* with you. You hear me? *Everywhere*. It's, like, voluntary." He sucked in his cheeks and turned to face me; his forehead was stippled from the mesh. "I want the key, Counselor. Give me the key. Give me the key now."

"Can't do it." I lit up a Marlboro despite the No Smoking sign. "Orders are orders."

Thompson studied me when the cannons started popping off again downriver. "You were over there, weren't you, Counselor?" He made a *gat-gat* sound with his tongue and his teeth. "You and me, Counselor," he said, "but we gonna get ours, ain't we? We gonna make a movie, using clay, tell everybody the truth." He picked up a thermoplastic chair and kicked it like a beachball. It skidded into the baseboard under the shatterproof glass of the nurse's station. "You and me, we don't belong here, Counselor." He got in my face, leaning close to the Zippo in my hand as though he wanted me to burn out his eyeballs. "How about a Marlboro for a piece of clay, Counselor?" He had a shank in one hand. A sharp-edged homemade knife. I gave him the lighter and the smokes. "There it is, Thompson," I said. "Back off." Instead, he reached into the pocket of my starched shirt and grabbed a carefully folded piece of paper.

The note was part of the ritual. Each day, I wrote to my girl-friend in Española, in New Mexico, where she taught children how to read. I clocked out each afternoon and took the bus down St. Claude, past swaybacked houses and unpainted shotgun shacks. I mailed my note at the letterbox outside the A&P in the Quarter, then walked home past the blind man who sat on the stoop of my apartment building.

Thompson pointed with his shank to the mesh. "It's an oven. Everytime I get free they turn up the heat and bake me like bread." He squeezed my collarbone.

A helicopter flew overhead, going downriver, and I squinted, grinding my jaw. "I told you to back off, Thompson." I crossed my arms. "Give me the note."

"Say please." He grinned and stubbed out his cigarette. "Say pretty please with a Marlboro on top."

"I'm not in the mood. Give it back."

"I'll trade you for the clay." He slipped his shank into a pocket and unfolded my note. "My, my," he mumbled, reading. "My, oh, my." He stared at me appraisingly. "She do that kind of thing for you?"

"Grow up, Thompson," I said.

"Sticks and bones," he said. "Electroshock, insulin coma, enough Thorazine kill a gorilla. None of that hurt *me*, Counselor. You-all tied me up three days and shot me with that new drug. You remember that? Who you think gonna pay the next twenty years while you fuck your piece of ass out in the world?" He turned his cap backward. The dog-ears flapped over his eyes. "You remember the machines? You were there, with the others. I was a piece of meat." He stalked away, still talking but out of my hearing, as though my senses were shutting down.

"Give me the note. And the shank. Put it on the table."

"You gonna make me, Counselor?"

Pacing, he flicked the Zippo and held it like a candle. His tennis shoes squeaked in rhythm with the outside squawks of river birds. "All my treasures, taken long ago," he said. "What's left? You think a smoke can buy me off?" He ripped off a salute. "What you don't know, Counselor, is that in a year, two, maybe five, I'm gonna look you up out in the world. You might not even remember me when your bell rings and you open your door, but I'm gonna clean your clock real good." He about-faced and I snatched the cap off his head. It was the color of army surplus. I planted it, still turned around, on my own head, and tucked the dog-ears away from my eyes, but Thompson didn't miss a beat. He didn't even notice. "Have faith. Counselor tells me have faith. In what, clay? You want me inside clay all the time? Microphones in the walls, circuits in my head. You have the nerve to preach about faith?" The woman on the television screamed at a man in a business suit. Cannon blasts downriver became intense again.

"All right, Counselor," I said, planting myself on the sofa in his favorite spot. "I'm you. What's next?"

Thompson puzzled over the switch. He squinted into the linoleum swirling around our feet, then reached in a pocket for a palmful of dehydrated peas. "You know Boudreaux pissed in the peas?" he said. "Like, I *ate* the peas, man, before I knew what that asshole was up to, so now I'm part Boudreaux's piss." He held out the peas. "I want these tested," he said. "Put these peas in your baggie." I did have a baggie, filled with vitamins and the occasional capsule from the nerve pill jar, and he knew it, so I tossed the peas in there with the vitamin C and the Librium. "It's a trade?" I said. "The peas for the note?"

He scratched the stubble on his cheek. He had the shank in his hand again, its blade razor-sharp.

"The note is personal, Thompson. Give it back."

"Shit on peas then." He stalked to the window mesh. "You call that freedom out there? Look at them wires. You know what it feels like, breathing high voltage, my tumor getting bigger every day?" He made his hands into fists, stared down at them. "That's why I have this tic douloureux. Electricity every goddamn day for weeks. *Boosh. Boosh.* Jump-starting my head like a goddamn automobile." He pointed the shank at me. "You get me out of here, Counselor." On the television, the woman's face contorted with betrayal as she held a phone to her ear. One of the guys in solitary screamed out something about the New Orleans Saints. Cannon blasts and musket fire were popping off like the Fourth of July. More helicopters passed overhead. The hospital became a listening post in-country. Rats scurried past. A firefight raged above me. I stitched together my brows and stared into the linoleum.

Then a squadron of jets roared close above us. They would be heading upriver. They would be tipping their wings. The Battle of New Orleans was over. "What the hell," I said. I tossed Thompson his cap. He held it by its well-thumbed visor. "War's over. Time to celebrate."

In the nurse's station, I opened a storage cabinet and lugged out a big dusty cardboard box filled with a thousand tiny packs of ketchup. A thousand therapeutic doses, I thought, enough ketchup in each pack to fill a syringe.

He snapped his fingers. "It's been a long time since Mardi Gras, man, a long time since I've had myself a beer on Decatur Street. Goddamn, I miss live music." He passed me the note. "Here's the ticket, man. What you got in mind?"

I pitched him a pack of ketchup. He used his cap like a scoop. Eyes electric, he stabbed the pack with the knife. I popped one myself. A circle of ketchup blistered my palm. Another pack, another dollop of ketchup, this time erupting like a bruise on my white shirt. On the warpath, I painted my face with ketchup. Thompson sucked in his cheeks, pinched his nose, and reached for more ketchup, the right side of his face palsied. He plastered his stubbled chin with ketchup and shaved, using the shank like a razor. The blade mowed away some of the stubble and also plowed through the skin with each tic of his face. He filled the nicks with ketchup, then stood on a thermoplastic chair and smeared the television screen until the soldiers on the midday movie disappeared in a fog of ketchup. He put the stuff everywhere. Stick men drawn on the nurse's shatterproof glass, ragged coins of ketchup on the dayroom walls, "FUCK YOU!" finger-painted on a door. He popped another pack, the kind they push through a bulletproof window at a fast-food joint. He leaned toward a catcher he could see who stood behind the window mesh. He studied the signs, wound up, and hurled a Nolan Ryan fastball. It splattered against the mesh, as though the high voltage was becoming visible. He struck out everyone he faced, with ketchup. He tossed the rest of the ketchup from the box, hundreds of rounds. He danced on ketchup, some weird dance with one foot in the air, face palsied again like a broken traffic signal. He squirted ketchup everywhere until the dayroom was a holy mess, ketchup smeared like paint or ink. It made sense to me and to Thompson. He was smiling, exhausted, gaptoothed, and full of goodwill. But it was one of those languages you make up as you go; the on-duty nurse, when she returned, would hardly understand or sympathize.

I picked up the shank, glinting red. I had cured him, I could see, cured him from the schizophrenia the chart said he had, but the place was a mess. I looked around the dayroom as though it was an X ray of my insides, as though I'd peeled away a layer or two of skin. All the blood and guts from the war were back and the whole place smelled like a diner. I turned my sticky palms to the television, where John Wayne was young and bristling with righteousness. It was the illusion of immortality all over again, as though I had descended into a listening-post tunnel and was swimming downstream, breathing through slits in my face.

Thompson rocked in his sneakers. When he flexed a wrist, snakelike scars of self-mutilation on the inside of his arm turned pale. His sneakers slid back and forth in the red grease with a sucking sound, his dog-eared hat forgotten on the tiles, ketchup drying on his stubbled cheeks. He stood at the nurse's window. "Don't have anything to do with an innocent victim, does it? You putting me on the cross, ain't you, man?" He talked into his reflection, su-perimposed over stick figures and the cluttered station. "Yeah, yeah, throw up your hands," he said. "I've suffered because of you." A computer screen blinked and the telephone rang. Thompson's chart hung from a clipboard like a slab of meat. There was an empty slot next to my plastic name on the wall, as though I was out to lunch or had never arrived.

I walked with the empty cardboard box and the knife past his flinty stare. As I washed up, he studied me silently, like an animal at the zoo, his brow puckered as though clearing the way for a new evolutionary idea.

CURED WITH KETCHUP I wrote on his chart.

Breathing in and out, the deep psychic space of the dayroom almost palpable, as though I could commune with everyone who had spent or wasted a life. I was certain those three words would explain everything even to the behaviorist and the social worker. I unbuttoned my shirt and left it on the nurse's swivel chair. The guy in solitary was shouting again, screaming out the lyrics to "When the Saints Go Marching In."

Thompson said, "I can throw clay and make you disappear!"

Outside, I waited in my T-shirt for the bus. I was no longer wearing a mask. When the kit and caboodle of patients and staff wheezed by in the hospital's old van, I caught a glimpse of a fedora, nodding up and down. At home, I found my pack, scrounged up a change of clothes, and caught a bus to Española. My girlfriend was surprised to see me, and not entirely happy, her late-night face full of cold cream and her underwear soaking in the tub. Even so, she listened until I talked myself hoarse. I told her about every fire-fight, every sucking chest wound, and every suckoff by every whore. She was a good and compassionate woman, and once I had been the face of her desire, but I quickly became the sadistic face of her misery.

"You have a low threshold of pain, don't you?" I said.

I returned to Louisiana, the Dream State. I figured that was where I belonged, back in New Orleans, where Mardi Gras and

Lent are yearlong obsessions. My last paycheck from the hospital was waiting, along with a letter of resignation the chief social worker expected me to sign. "If you need a recommendation, let me know," her note advised, "and try not to drink so much." Instead of signing the letter, I applied for unemployment benefits, and after a hearing received a regular check in the mail. It was odd, not working. I lived in my shabby apartment above Royal Street in a kind of fever, so much time for discipline, so much for dissipation. Though the calculus was interior and complex, one thing was for certain. My career as a psychological aide was history, another revolving door. But I kept reading the books they had forced upon me. *Feeling Good. Reality Therapy.* I read other books as well, very different books about a man turning into a dung beetle and another man, impotent, falling in love with a promiscuous femme fatale. And each evening, when the sun went down and the blistered streets finished braising, I put down my book or my bottle and walked Fred, the blind man, to the crowded aisles of the A&P. It was my one obligation. He always wanted something spicy, like barbecued potato chips or pickled okra. Back on our stoop, chewing on his snack with delight, facing the street in his dark owlframes and greasy hat, he would listen to me. He was the only person on the face of the earth who listened to what I had to say. I talked about the tourists who gawked at everything on their way to Bourbon Street or the locals who loitered in doorways and sat on spiderwork balconies fanning themselves. I made him laugh.

It was a life I might have lived forever, a schizophrenic's life, but one hot night when I couldn't sleep the jazz from nearby Preservation Hall filtered through my window. Thompson floated into my head like a sapper, his tic douloureux keeping wild rhythm with the jazz. "What's wrong with clay?" he said, scatting out the words, drumming them into my head. "You got something against the Vietnamese?" He snapped his fingers, his turned-around cap clamped over his eyes. "What's wrong with ketchup? You don't like green peas?"

My room became a listening post. Faces filed past.

Asleep, I spat them out like trinkets. The smell of ketchup was everywhere. It was the only dream I've ever had with an odor to it. I tried to hold fast to the dream, stay with the smell of the jazz, read it like a book, but the light came through my bare window and I was afraid not to open my eyes.

I walked hungover to Jackson Square, where I sat on a wrought iron bench under a palm tree. Street artists were setting up their easels around the square. Andrew Jackson, the savior of New Orleans, was rearing up on the oldest equestrian statue in the country. He was tipping his hat, freshly scrubbed of pigeon droppings. Homeless people were getting rousted from under planks of cardboard and blankets of old newspaper and stumbling into the new day, holding out their hands and mumbling.

A few came my way, but I had nothing to give them. "I'm going to the river," I said. "Come along if you want." One told me to go get fucked. "Not a bad idea," I said, but an emaciated man wearing a Saints T-shirt came with me and we talked the way people in New Orleans do, just passing the time. Every step we took was awkward and painful, because he was full of rheumatism and because one of my legs was asleep. I couldn't wake it up, but we helped each other over the levee and sat together near the water for a long time, listening to how a big river moves.

When a tanker's whistle shrieked a stone's throw away, the old man stood up. He was permanently tilted to one side after too many nights of sleeping on pavement, but he started swaying and then I could hear taps on his shoes click on the concrete until the sound he made with his feet had something to do with those sweet circles of ketchup that had cured Thompson of schizophrenia.

He danced for me a long time, and when he was finished I nodded and smiled and pulled out my empty pockets so that he could see I had nothing to give him. He went off in the direction of the Aquarium, whose glass sides glinted in the bright sun, and I spent the rest of the morning and most of the afternoon staring into the brown and silty water rushing past me, hearing conversations in my own language and in languages that did not and never would belong to me. Then I listened to the water that seemed bright like metal in the afternoon glare and it was discipline and not dissipation. It was easy to imagine myself on board one of the monster freighters that wailed on its way downriver. I thought about where it had been and where it might find itself, in the Gulf of Mexico, in the ocean, on the other side of the world, and who knows, maybe back again, and it was all ketchup and I was using it.

BEAUTY OF TROPICAL PLACES

My brother Roy, a priest, called long distance late the other night. We don't talk much anymore, so it was odd for him to use me as a sounding board. But seven years after his ordination he's fallen in love, despite his vocation, despite his vow of celibacy. "Dan, I'm calling you from my office in the rectory," he said. "I feel like a criminal." He's associate pastor now in a large parish in North Dakota, and from my San Francisco apartment I can see him there at his crowded desk with the window open to the night wind, paperweights holding everything down. The Christ whose eyes follow you anywhere you move hangs in resurrected piety on the beige office wall, arms spread wide to the world. It's the Christ given to Roy by our devout aunt Mary on his First Communion, the low Christ, he likes to complain, as opposed to the high Christ, who is more contemplative than orthodox.

"Nobody's *listening*. You've got to *listen*, Dan." He met her on retreat, a weekend for singles. He was retreat master. "I was at the center to counsel people who've been too long alone. Some of these women are widows, you understand, Dan, coming out of bad marriages, with or without annulments. Cissie lived for years with a man who told her one night he wanted her to leave. She was still in love with him when we met. She's had a lot of pain in her life." He stopped talking and the phone clunked to his desk. I could hear a muffled sound and I wondered whether he was crying.

Our talks have always been punctuated by elisions, by backtracking and apologies for opinions too baldly stated. The Christ with ketchup in his beard, I used to tease, pointing to the uplifted eyes, the pastel robe with its splotches of cherry blood, getting Roy's goat as he prepared with prayer and grooming for altar boy duties. "The oblations must be taken seriously," he'd say, bending close to the mirror like James Dean primping for the cameras. I'd pull open the centerfold of a secret *Playboy* and describe its charms for him. "Life is a fiction," I would say, a college sophomore three years his senior itching for philosophical debate, "except for the body. It's hard to get past a dead body on a slab. A piece of meat." I was deep into Hemingway. "It's hard to ignore what your body wants when you're with the right woman."

Outside in the moonlight, great avocados hung like ghostly green bells from my landlady's backyard tree. Along with Theresa, until recently my longtime companion, I was addicted to the beauty of tropical places, to sunlight. We had lived most of the year in the sun. The smell of jasmine and oranges made Fargo, North Dakota, nearly impossible to imagine. "I should have been a monk," Roy said. "A hermit monk, safe from temptation."

"Fat chance," I said. "Look at Merton. The longer he lived as a monk did, the more he wanted the world. He almost left the monastery for a woman. You didn't know that, did you?" I gulped down half a cup of coffee and poured more from the thermos on my desk. "He would have been better off as a Graham Greene, somebody lost and coming to himself in a new place." I laughed. "Or a beatnik in a hippie commune."

"Well, you're the man of the world," Roy said, refusing to take the bait. He meant all the drinking I used to do, my forgetting that love existed. He meant my bitter divorce and the child I saw on holidays. He meant Theresa. She was as alienated from the worka-day world as I imagined myself to be. Most of the year, we had sub-leased our apartment back East and lived like gypsies, looking for offbeat beauty, Europe in the summer when we could afford it, New Orleans when Manhattan grew chilly. "Most people don't know how to live," Theresa said once as she tragically sipped café au lait and munched beignets at the Café du Monde in the Quarter, surrounded by tourists in bright skirts and blouses, the *clop-clop* of draft horses pulling buggies, the sour fishy odor of the Mississippi. Her eyes, the dark excited eyes of a seal, turned on me with rapture. "Too many people keep their eyes cast to the ground," she said. "We're very fortunate to have found one another. Most people never follow their bliss." She reached out for my hand, as though we were united in a kind of awe by our luck.

"Look, Roy," I said, "I'm sorry. Talk to me. I'm listening." In San Francisco, I teach part-time and freelance to make ends meet. "What's it like up there in Fargo?"

"Ordinary time." He did a lot of counseling in his office, and I knew there was a picture of our family on a table between two chairs. As we spoke, he could stare from his desk at my bearded face. I stood beside my mother with one hand on her shoulder. "Travel Light & Travel Fast," my T-shirt said in crimson. "Everybody high-tails it out of town to the lakes for the weekend once it gets hot. You hear your voice echo at Mass." He took an audible breath. "On Pentecost I felt like a jerk, telling people about tongues of fire, about speaking in tongues. I stood in the sacristy after Mass, wringing my hands, wanting to touch her."

"So," I said, "you've got it bad, huh?" Sitting at my own small desk, I pushed aside a stack of final papers, each an explication of "A Clean Well-Lighted Place," and found a pad of paper.

"*Listen,*" he said, "please. Aren't you *listening?*" I heard the *tap-tap* of his coffee mug on his desk. "I've had a lot of funerals in the last few weeks. A lot of people are dying up here."

"I'm sorry," I said. "Talk to me, Roy." I could see the yellow sandwich boards—NO PARKING, FUNERAL TODAY—along the curb in front of the stone church. Roy had presided at a funeral during my last visit—a twenty-year-old man killed in a hunting accident. Quite coincidentally, we went for beers after the funeral to a place called the Hunter and Trapper, the walls hung with pelts and the heads of deer. It was hard to speak to him plainly, then or now, as though I could affirm my identity only by wandering while he stayed put. I remembered how much his celibacy had once offended me. I persuaded a stripper, a college girl, to hide in his dorm room and jump out once he undressed. She had round supple breasts and the firm muscular thighs of a cheerleader. I had a tape recorder going under the bed. "You're great looking," my brother told the naked girl casually, the tape scratchy, afflicted with odd noises. "Do you know about Saint Agatha? She's the patron saint of breasts." She giggled like a good old girl, somebody's sweetheart, and didn't try to touch him. She respected him, she told me later, dressed demurely in a blue dress with a string tie. "You ought to be glad to have a priest in the family," she said. "That's his way. You ought to show respect."

It's just a face he puts on, I tried to convince her, but I was old enough by then to know better. I even wanted it to be possible, that kind of steadfastness. "Roy, I still think life is fiction," I said, "and I still have trouble getting past the body, but sometimes, from the corner of my eye, I sense how much I don't know, how lost we can be without hope." I drank more coffee and Roy poured out his guts into that piece of plastic into my ear. He said he still believed in Christ, whose eyes follow you everywhere. "Life *is* fiction," he said, "but it's grounded in Christ. After Christ, anything is possible. Christ writes the world. The Bible is the great book about living in but letting go of the world. I'm not deserting God when I think about being with Cissie. It's the Church I'd have to leave."

I tried to listen, but the aroma of oranges and jasmine outside my window got me seeing an old mill near Savannah covered over with kudzu, Theresa wading toward it, thigh-deep in kudzu. I remembered the rustle of honeysuckle on a porch in New Orleans, tasted the wine I drank there with Theresa before we caught a plane for the Caribbean and a month in Martinique.

The only doodle on my pad was a stick figure with big bug eyes holding a spear. I put some ground under its feet and a big sun in the sky, a mountain on the horizon. Roy was asking me again whether I was listening, whether anything he said made any kind of sense. I told him I remembered him lying prostrate before the altar at his ordination, promising obedience, trust, and respect. The bishop talked about compassion, told Roy to have it but to keep it under control with common sense. The bishop and the priests laid their hands on Roy, then vested him with the chasuble, a sleeveless garment, and the stole, a long linen scarf. "You were a priest, Roy. I didn't know what to make of that. I still don't. You believe completely in God, in that Christ on the wall I used to tease you about."

"Dan, I'm going away for a week with Cissie, up to the Boundary Waters. We have to talk about what I want, what I think I want, what I really want. She knows the trouble I'd be, a man not really at home anywhere in the world, not very good at practical things. I keep a garden but it's mostly sleight of hand. People come in when I'm not paying attention and pull the weeds, do what I forget about. I don't know how to repair a leaky faucet, how to use one of those levels with that little bubble to tell you when something is straight."

"A whiskey priest is still a priest," I said.

There was silence on Roy's end.

"Anyway, you could be with her and still be a man of the cloth, couldn't you, if you went to another church?"

"I can't just change churches the way you—" He caught himself, cleared his throat. "I'm sorry, Dan, you and I disagree about everything, but I'm still terrified of disappointing you. You're still my big brother. I *need* to tell you all of this. I need you to *listen*."

"Look, Roy, I've lived through a lot of trouble myself. There was the divorce, all that breakup, but I thought Theresa was my soulmate, someone to live with forever. I thought it was what God intended, if you don't mind me putting it that way." I had been swept away, and Theresa was ecstatic. "All this dark wood," she said in a German restaurant in Chicago, "a fairy-tale forest." At the Art Institute she wrote voluptuously in her notebooks while standing before a series of small, haunting portraits in which Ivan Albright, a dying artist, recorded his physical dissolution, his wasting away to nothing, but who, even at the end, in quavering pencil instead of bright oils, managed shaky deathbed portraits. In the restaurant, over red wine and bratwurst, she shook her head in disbelief at the hectic noontime crowd. "Don't they know they're going to die?"

A year ago, shortly after our move to the Bay area, she recalled that Chicago afternoon and Albright. "Let's go to France," she said. "There's a colony there for artists. Let's spend this winter in the mountains of France. We're getting old. It's so beautiful there."

For a second, though the feeling passed quickly, and though I immediately reached out to her and held her tightly, I wanted to strangle her. That way, we both would have to stay in one place.

She went without me, not to France but back to Martinique to have a month alone. We both had affairs. I got involved with a strapping blond who had a goofy sense of humor. Theresa met a wanderer, and with the last of her savings rented a beachfront cottage for the two of them.

I told Roy all of this, more or less, and he gave me his blessing.

I remembered it was Sunday. "The Lord's day," I said. "When Mom was alive, Sunday was always the Lord's day. The Lord. The Lord. All I ever heard about on Sunday was the Lord."

"Yes," Roy said, "I remember that." He told me he had an early Mass and needed a little rest. He told me he would call me back when he and Cissie returned from the lakes.

I thought about going to church that day, but the Cubs were playing the Giants at Candlestick Park. I went to the stadium and sat above the third-base line, studying the ball game for some kind of clue, something I could say to Roy the next time he called. It came in the fifth inning, halfway through the game, when a batter for the Cubs lofted a long, lazy flyball. The outfielder drifted back, squinting and holding his breath; then he broke toward the foul line on the run, his glove outstretched. He dove for the ball and for a moment was flying above the ground, reaching with every muscle, but the ball, which seemed to have a mind of its own, landed just beyond his reach, perhaps inches fair, and rolled to the fence. The outfielder thudded into the ground and dislocated a shoulder; the batter ended up at third base. For the rest of the game, the image of that man, floating, stayed with me, and thinking of him made me think of my brother. Nobody ever quite knows how to play such a ball, I thought I could tell him, or where it might land, because anything is possible, anything might happen, when a man is horizontal to the ground as though levitating in the beauty of a tropical place.

THE VANISHING

The cat continued to bring home birds and place them in the water dish, their wings spread across its bottom. It ate the food I left for it when I slept and brought the birds inside through a flap in the bottom of the door that faced out back. In my dreams, birds cawed and flapped until they drowned, and so I would wake and gaze into the mirror and see my hair going away. I called it the vanishing, the latest disappearing act. My father from Scotland was gone, my mother his keeper was gone, my marriage had exploded into smithereens, and now I was losing my hair. I still had clumps of it over either ear, like tufts of gray weed unmowed because the machine couldn't get to it, but except for a blackhead the top of my scalp glared like a ski slope.

Keeping my sense of humor, I thought I might sell lift tickets.

I knew about a lotion I could slather on, a pill I could take, but I didn't kid myself. It was about life and death, a plain object that my eyes could see.

I went to the kitchen for coffee and found another bird visible through clear water in the drinking dish. It was on its back, neck broken, feathers slick.

There was a place around the corner next to the cemetery where my father was buried that sold hair. It was a procedure I could see myself prosecuting with absolutely firm logic: get a rug, glue it on, smile, but for years I had woven myself not with strands of hair but with thoughts. When I saw that day how bald I was, I also noticed how lines cratered my eyes and surrounded my mouth. I remembered how my wife took hold of the vanishing as a weapon when we tangled. The object I had possessed, a vision of my own omnipotence, had been one that shielded me like an umbrella from the deep knowing, from her ancient Gnostic energy that swerved around me like lightning and thunder until the marriage exploded and she packed a suitcase and left.

It was my intention, when she went away, to reconstitute myself. After she left, I was not a consumer but a project; at least, I was not the kind of consumer who buys hair.

I knew enough to know that it was a range of motion I needed.

I tried to sustain a new thing with motion in mind. I exercised, but the range of motion I needed was not calisthenics. "No pain, no gain," my personal trainer said, but there was no magic in side-straddle hops. I tried rigorously employing my logic, but that did not work either. I tried spectator sports, golf, pornography, the web, coffee clubs, cigars, wine tasting, working overtime. I even took a lesson on becoming a clown. "You're not the type," the instructor said. It was like projecting a feeble image on a pane of glass.

My range of motion was circumscribed and suspect.

I began to think that there might not be a *there* there. I could see where I needed to go, what had to be inscribed, but I couldn't get to it.

It was about then that I took up the bagpipe.

I came across one on sale at a charity bazaar and bought it outright. It was not agleam in its glory on the scarred table where it lay deflated under a blanket of dust. It was dull like silverware before being burnished. There was no box for it and so I had to carry it through the bazaar. "Hey, mister, let me hear you swing," a kid with snot on his nose said. I tried, made a goon of myself, but couldn't get out a single note. Even in my scantness, though, I liked pumping the windbag and tonguing the blowpipe.

I found a woman to give me lessons. "It'll cost," she said. She was good and I was fast.

At night, in my flat, my range of motion improved, but the sound was still hideous, something like the screech of a bird, and so I took it to the cemetery. The drone pipe and chanter became weapons of choice against the vanishing. I would walk (though not in kilts) to my father's grave with my bagpipe and blow myself silly standing over it. "Hey, Dad, how you like these apples?" I would ask, taking a jaunty tone, but he never replied. As I rocked from foot to foot, the tassels whipped around and the stock inlaid with gold reflected sunlight on clear days, though it was best when I played at night.

The cat liked to skulk in the ruins and sometimes when I couldn't sleep I could hear it howl at the moon. I would rise up and blow. Each time I practiced, it became easier to keep up the range of motion by forgetting about the vanishing. When I played, especially in the cemetery, I would let go and descend, if I was lucky, into a dream of transfiguration, a gaze that stayed within itself. The gravestones around me glistened under the moon like rune stones in Scotland. My playing became an incantation of mysterious significance that called the cat to me. It would prowl on the periphery of my father's grave in moonlight. My world became a secret world, never known in the days when my father walked the earth. My mother rested a rune's distance from where I stood, and I liked to think that my utterances were no longer words but the plosives of my bagpipe whirling from rune to rune so that the mysterious magic of epitaphs somehow mingled with the notes that I played.

Was my song feeble or potent?

I have never been able to answer that question, and as I play I can't tell, but I know that I knew how to write on the body, even the body of my father beneath me that had turned so quickly to dust. I knew that I could die without my hair, standing on my father's grave I knew that, but dying is only a bodily experience and I knew that, too. If I can die, I thought, then why not play the bagpipes until I do?

My cat came up to me as my song echoed from grave to grave. It dropped a dead, ruffled bird at my feet.

ALONE WITH THE OWL

In his cell, Howard kept the image of the owl before him as he crossed off each day on his calendar; he had plenty of time to figure how a lanky black outfielder called up one September by the Cubs could find himself, only a couple of years down the road, planning and carrying out a minor-league holdup. He remembered the last home run he ever hit, the trot around the bases after the ball sailed over the fence into the piney woods where the hootowl lived. Touching home plate, thinking he could still call up his old power, he had allowed his gaze to sweep away from the piney woods through near-empty bleachers to a '58 Chevy up on blocks.

He planned the robbery sitting in his apartment at a wobbly window desk, where he penciled out a crude captioned map of the convenience store. *Enter here, exit here, park getaway car in back, this route to interstate.* The moon was rising over the piedmont of North Carolina, even though it was still daylight. The sun was setting even as the moon rose, as though the world was coming to an end. The millennium. To his outfielder's eyes, fading but still good enough to study the spin of the seams on a hanging curve, sun and moon appeared the same size, and his neck, arthritic at thirty, was the pivot on a cosmic scale from which he could not escape.

He did several versions of each map, seeing the problem in his mind and refining his thoughts, rehearsing the scene and working out contingencies, throwing scraps of paper on the floor, using a straightedge on the last version. *Step one*, he wrote. *Plunge knife into counter.* That way the clerk will see the knife and nothing else. *Step two. Tell clerk to empty cash drawer. Say nothing else. Disguise voice. Talk mechanically like a robot.*

He broke open a bottle of Jack Daniel's. He didn't particularly want to add to the world's vast store of meanness, but the thought of making some quick money in a world that plotted against him was a challenge.

Besides, what difference did it make? Afterward, trying to explain it to Hassie, his ex-wife, so that she could tell Sally, their daughter, some version of what had come to pass, he told her that he had dreamed of a quick score, of catching up on his child-support payments. After a life devoted to a Louisville Slugger and a Rawlings, futile grabs for the brass ring of the big leagues, he had nothing but a rented apartment, a few sticks of ragtag furniture, a photograph of Hassie and Sally embracing him from all angles on a long-ago Father's Day, and a lunatic notion that he could exact revenge in the time-honored tradition of highway robbery.

Talking to Hassie, he blamed it on the wooden owl with detachable wings that hung like a mobile from the ceiling above Sally's bed. He often dreamed of the owl, he told Hassie, the same dream, the owl alive but unmoving amid chaos like a grave on a windy night. Its large wooden eyes stared at the bedroom door. Sally was fast asleep, whimpering to some shadow-figure that wanted to do her damage, and Howard, hovering over the house where he no longer lived, could sense Hassie's featherweight breath in the next room. The owl's painted wings rustled like feathers, as though made of pillow stuff instead of balsa. Its eyes, obsidian deep, gray gone to shiny black, were fractured, prismatic, but missed nothing. Howard knew it was fiercely protective of his family and would attack any creature, human or otherwise, who tried to harm Sally.

"There's no wooden owl," Hassie told him. She was staring at him strangely. "Forget that owl. For the life of me, I have no idea what you mean, and no reasonable body can make sense of it. You're imagining it. You never gave Sally an owl or nothing like it. I can't even guess what you're thinking."

"No matter what you say. That owl had something to do with the stickup," he told her. "It explains what happened better than I can myself. I dreamed about that owl, baby, I was flying with it, I was the owl, and I woke up thinking I'd make myself into an owl, fly off with enough to keep you-all off welfare."

"We were never on welfare," Hassie said, scratching her fingernails into the wooden table between them. "I always made more money than you did. Your baseball money was never a big deal. Maybe you ought to plead insanity."

The moon had risen, flavoring his maps with moonshine, and the sun had dipped below the horizon. Still working on the whiskey, staring stupidly at the maps, he saw his own mind reflected in the moonlight slanted across his secondhand desk. Clouds and sheet lightning moved in. What knotty pine, Howard wondered, did the owl inhabit when it rained? He glanced one last time at his maps and made a cup of freeze-dried coffee, sweetened New Orleans fashion with sugar and whiskey and plenty of rich milk. Then he went outside and stood in the rain, hating himself because he was going to force a convenience store clerk to his knees. He had been held up himself once when he worked at an A&W rootbeer stand in New Orleans. Temporarily alone in the store, he had looked up from the shake machine into a small pistol quavering in the kid's hand. Without speaking, the kid gave him a greasy paper bag. Howard emptied the till into it without a moment's hesitation. It wasn't his money. Satisfied, the kid motioned him to the floor with the pistol and leaned over the counter. "*Bam!* You stay there, you okay. You get up, you dead."

Howard did as he was told, breathing in floorwax and the dust of greasy linoleum. Then he called the cops and waited, staring into one of those long sloe-eyed New Orleans evenings. Cars still jockeyed for lane position on Veteran's Highway, the sun burned its vapors over the swamps west of Jefferson Parish, and kids stopped at the A&W to lollygag, but none of it was real anymore. He waved out the kids who happened into the store—"Cops on the way, trouble here." He felt as empty as a person could get without deflating. He hated the job anyway—it was what he did one off-season, waiting to get back into the minors.

When the cops arrived, he bluffed his way through their questions, but he couldn't remember whether the kid was wearing a black T-shirt and sneakers or a button-down plaid shirt and thrift-store oxfords. The cops questioned him for a long time and he understood that he was a suspect; it was only when the manager arrived and vouched for him that they finished their interrogation and let him be. What he still remembered was the gun quavering in his face with one nervous finger on the trigger; the gun was lopsided somehow, as though it had been used mostly to hammer nails.

In the rain he finished his coffee. Already trees were bowing to the dry clap of thunder. There was lightning over the piedmont. A great wall of water was approaching, a thunderhead as inevitable as the robbery. He saw it that night as his fate, as though the universe was in motion with him aboard for the ride. He exulted in the prospect of Armageddon. Somewhere, some unreformed Baptist saw the same rain and thought how something would burn. A drunk somewhere took cover under a protective overhang at a seedy Salvation Army shelter and saw the light in the storm and was saved, but there was no salvation for Howard, especially since the convenience store in Knoxville stayed open twenty-four hours a day. He and Legat, his accomplice, a catcher bombed out and stranded in the bush leagues but too dumb to admit it, would do the deal. Walk in like Tut, take from the corporations that exploit their workers, and buzz off a thousand bucks richer. The store's location, on Tuckaseegee Road near the interstate, made the getaway easy. Steal a license plate, keep the car out of sight. Steal a car. There was no real reason to pick that particular convenience store, but there it was.

After all, he told Hassie, justifying his stupidity even when there was no point, jerks make the law, other jerks dance cheek-to-cheek with lawmakers. Fat-cat politicians line their pockets, spout their jive every which way, suits and ties throw round their money to get the laws they want, bully cops at a slow burn look out for graft and beat up on the brothers, hordes of businessmen have nothing in mind but raw accumulation.

"Don't make it worse," Hassie said. "Don't talk like an idiot and add to your troubles. Right now, it looks like you get off easy. First offense, no weapon, though that copy of *Muhammad Speaks* they found in the car won't help matters none. Besides, you're not speaking to some drunk in a bar. You're talking to me, and I would just like to hear you give me an explanation that makes sense."

Afterward, it was too late for sense, and Howard could think of nothing to say. Hassie refused to leave him to his fate, came to see him on a regular basis, but he only had the one story to tell, and tell her he must. He muttered something about the owl that he was dead-sure he had given to his daughter, but it was not an object that meant anything at all to Hassie; Howard himself wasn't sure how to put into words the owl's importance. Without that creature of prey on his mind, without its feathered talons and large forward-set eyes, there would have been no holdup, of that he was certain, but the corollary to such a notion was that he would have no hope in prison if he couldn't carry with him day and night a vision of a creature whose fluffy plumage permitted silent flight and ceaseless witness.

He had put down the cup of coffee and gone off running in the rain, feet churning as though beating out a slow grounder. The ballpark had once been his sanctuary and he still found his way to it when he needed a boost. Muscle memory. It was the ballpark where he had played on his way up to the bigs and it was the ball-park where he was playing on the roller-coaster ride down. He ran through the rain past it and headed for Legat's apartment. He ran past rundown frame houses with sagging front porches and mon-grels tied to unpainted posts. But the neighborhood had changed, houses converted into townhouses, apartments into condos. Soon, real estate would be too valuable to waste and the ballpark, along with the piney woods behind it, would go the way of the drive-in theater on the edge of town, sacrificed to progress and the Cham-ber of Commerce, which was promoting a project to build a slick new stadium with all the class of an aluminum bat. The town no longer considered itself minor-league.

Legat was from out East, Brooklyn. Howard, from the tough Ninth Ward in New Orleans, took an instant liking to him. Howard had the brains, Legat that wild omnivorous look that scared the hell out of people. They wouldn't need a gun.

The cards get read and you do what you need to do, he thought that night when he completed his plan. It was an exhilarating feeling to give himself over to something besides baseball. He stood under the flat tin roof on Legat's upstairs porch and rousted the catcher. The two of them drove through the neighborhood to a bar on the edge of town. Howard could feel the neighborhood around him, the psychic density of people living face-to-face on their wits and weekly wages while yuppies, like the one who took Hassie from him, used their money to take over the neighborhood, rehab it, replace old taverns with fern bars.

"It's a crime," he said, "what they do. What we do is nothing compared to that." He was driving Legat's old Chevrolet. Legat was too drunk to drive. Howard was tempted to keep driving, past the amusement park on the edge of town into the Deep South, past places where George Wallace was still a hero, where right-to-work was still a sacred Baptist ritual right up there with communion and holy matrimony, all the way to the coastal plain, to Mobile, Biloxi, and New Orleans, to the palm trees and banana trees and the steam-bath humidity that might cleanse his every pore. Legat was dozing, out for the ride but not up to it, and Howard's own manic energy dissolved quickly enough into an alcoholic stupor. It was the middle of the month and there was a full moon, but all he could see was rain. How many chances had he wasted because the only thing he cared about was the bigs?

Afterwards, trying to piece it together, Hassie studying his face, his time with her running out, he could remember trotting home in the rain, his knees protesting each wrench. Soaking wet and loving it, screaming out at the top of his lungs, he could remember collecting his maps, finishing the bottle of Jack Daniel's in the rain, circling the block and heading back to the ballpark. After the storm, he could remember carving out designs in the dry-rotted wooden grandstand replete with jigsaw scrollwork reminiscent of wrought iron in the French Quarter. He trotted around the bases on the tarp in rhythm to distant receding claps of thunder. He climbed the light tower for no reason, swayed high above the field as the only competitor in some odd contest, the landscape around him still illuminated with shafts of lightning. After he came down, he went to the outfield and dug out huge divots of grass and soil with a stick, but he couldn't remember what had happened that night to Legat. Had he forgotten him at the bar? They both looked at the world through the eyes of kids brought up on the wrong side of the tracks, and they both liked to get totally wasted as often as they could. They must have been wasted that night. He could remember how the sky cleared and kicked into fast forward. A blur of darkness, then a band of red visible out east. It was cockcrow and the day became sunny and sweet with the smell of camellias and azaleas and myrtle blossoms, but he had been soggy and hungover and the world had felt like an appendix about to burst.

"Anyway," he told Hassie, "there was another bar where Legat and I hung out the night of the stickup. It was called Eve's Place." It was one of those dives near the interstate on the outskirts of Knoxville. The few regulars looked like parolees or serial murderers, eyes lost, searching for a victim or a cause. One or two looked his way every now and then like they wanted to start something, but then they looked at Legat and decided to mind their own business. Everyone was crazy bitter about something, Howard no different, and the bitterness was sweet when it was nursed over shots and chasers. You could hardly see the eight ball for the smoke, and the whole place smelled like beer, sawdust, and cheap bourbon. A woman with nice legs and a horsey face was dancing, mostly for her own amusement, on a dimly lit mirrored stage at one end of the bar, and every so often Howard looked at her real good. He had his maps with him, worked up by now with the precision of a draftsman, and he had Legat liquored up.

"We're four point eight miles from the convenience store," Howard said to Legat. When he stood up, the blood rushed to his head. Something by Mick Jagger that nobody bothered to listen to was on the jukebox. Man ought to give it up, become a producer or change his sex, get a face-lift and sit behind a big desk somewhere counting other people's money. Man didn't know when to stop.

Should have been shot like Sam Cooke so people could remember him young and handsome, at the top of his charm.

By the time they got around to talking about their plan for the night, the place was crowded and noisy, the strippers more lively, so Howard sat Legat down in a smoky back room, out of sight of the strippers. The room was deserted except for a drunk with stringy hair and gaunt shoulder blades who stared at his reflection in a broken television set. Howard ordered two pitchers of beer and a big plate of nachos. "Dig in, Legat." He pulled his maps from his back pocket, uncrinkled them, laid them in the center of the table, and detailed his plan, all the while keeping their glasses topped. After dozens of revisions, his maps were color-coded (red highways, black highways, blue highways) and marked with points of interest, main thoroughfares, block numbers, directional arrows, mileage indicators, route numbers, and even used-car lots.

"What about the cyanide pills?" Legat said. He mumbled under his breath and stared wildly around the room. He looked like a vicious parody of a blue-collar beer commercial—work done for the day, bonding time with his mates. He put his knobby fingers down on the table. "You want me to listen? I'm listening."

Afterward, Howard told Hassie the only weapon he had with him was a plastic fork from a fast-food restaurant, but that was not entirely true. There was a Louisville Slugger in his trunk, and Legat had a pellet gun and an extension cord. They also had a box of garbage bags to use as masks. But there had been no knife to plunge into the counter. Somehow, he and Legat forgot completely about the knife. Somehow, they forgot to switch license plates, a piece of carelessness that made all the difference.

At the bar, Howard studied the tiny tattoo of a whooping crane on the underside of his right arm. Flexing his wrist made the wings and long stick legs move. "You know the score," he said to Legat, who seemed more interested in the nachos. "You know what kind of shape your knees are in, how your fingers feel every morning, how your back aches when you swing the bat." He flexed his wrist and pointed to the maps. "Nothing can go wrong. I'm talking robbing from the rich and giving to the poor. I'm talking Robin Hood."

"Yeah, right." Legat finished his pitcher of beer. "If we're going to do it," he said, "don't bullshit me, let's just do it."

Outside, a red neon sign blinked on and off, waxing the car and transforming Legat's face into a garish celluloid caricature of a mob hitman. He looked as hard-boiled as the bikers and drifters still boozing inside. The night was a beauty, the sky star-filled. Howard remembered such nights at the ballpark, when lights would halo the heavens and the beaver *thwack* of fungoes would fill the air. Outside Eve's, he took a leak in bushy leaf-haunted shadow, thinking that Legat looked like somebody who could have crawled out of the hills with a shotgun and a thirst for the good things in life, like cockfights and gang rapes.

"We're one bad pair of mothers," Howard said, clowning. He hitched up his pants and fell into a jiveass routine. He could barely see Legat. So much was so dark, the lighting low-key, the night smudged up close, but distant objects like billboards and roadhouse signs were clear as crystal. Eve's door under the buglight, painted in coarse-grained stripes to look antique, was vivid, but he couldn't make out even a glint of light in the concrete drainage coulee a few feet from where he stood, though he could hear water gurgle like a man gasping for air.

As they drove, Howard felt his muscles betray him, his heart beat madly. He should have specified that they would never pull the job drunk. His stomach was sinking. Something real was going to happen away from the ballfield. Until now, baseball had been everything, but for the rest of his life he would be doomed to be someone different from who he was. An insomniac by nature, he often stayed up, drinking his spiked coffee. When morning came, he would jog for the morning paper with its box scores and study the bigs over more coffee. He would look for a player who was hot and think about that player, how he waited in the on-deck circle or swung the bat, how he dug in or held back with the count against him. He would meditate like a monk, clearing his mind like an overgrown garden of all extraneous detail before the game. Then, in the on-deck circle himself, he would live inside his meditation, stay within himself.

He pulled into the lot of the convenience store on the I-40 access road. The fast-fare places around it were closed for the night. He parked the car next to a Dumpster behind the store. Hand inside a plastic garbage bag, he checked the back door. It was unlocked. He and Legat poked out slits in garbage bags with the handle of the plastic fork. They fitted themselves with the disguises, like a group of adolescents who refused to outgrow Halloween. Howard crept around the building to the front of the store, verified that there were no customers, only bright fluorescence and orderly shelves. The clerk, white-shirted back facing Howard, was restocking the frozen dinners and microwave sandwiches. The service road was completely empty in both directions and brightly lit, as though the apocalypse was about to occur and the strip was prepared for an influx of scarred, mutilated victims, every one hungry for junk food.

Behind the store, Howard stepped over the glassy splinters of a broken beer bottle and motioned Legat inside. They entered the storage room to the surflike rustle of the garbage bags. In the customer area beyond a curtain, the clerk was still pumping TV dinners into the freezer compartment. "He'll come back here when the box is empty," Legat whispered.

Howard was having trouble breathing. He made a larger tear in the bag and squinted past bits of black plastic. The uneven slit restricted his field of vision, as though his retina was torn and the world was a play of light and shadow. Almost in panic, he pushed aside the curtain, turned the corner, and grabbed the clerk from behind. "This is a holdup," he said, and felt silly, but he made his voice as thick and mechanical as he could. "We're not armed. We are *not* armed. Do *not* turn around." He felt awkward with the plastic bag over his head and gripped the clerk's upper arms tightly. Both hands occupied, he couldn't adjust his breathing slit and found himself gasping for air. "Into the back," he said, and blew out, as though inflating a balloon, to get the plastic away from his mouth.

Legat emerged into the glare. The clerk stared in their direction. "Keep your head down," Howard ordered. "Nobody gets hurt."

"Jesus Christ," Legat said. "It's a girl." Legat had the white plastic fork in one hand and was eating an animal cookie with the other, shoveling it through the mouth-hole in his garbage bag.

The clerk's high-pitched hysterical giggle caused Legat to drop the cookie in alarm. "Look," the clerk said, making an effort to keep her head down, "I get minimum wage. Take what you want. If you-all want, take everything." She spoke carefully, enunciating each syllable like a kindergarten teacher, her drawl emphasizing the last word in each sentence. "I could care less. Really. It's all yours."

Howard felt a frog in his throat, thought of Sally, and nearly choked. He could feel, now, the girlish muscle in her upper arms, the hunch of her shoulder blades, the baby-fine hair on the nape of her neck. "The register," he mumbled, his voice low. "The money," he said to Legat, and marched the girl into the back room.

He sat her facing the wall on a box filled with bottles of reconstituted lemon juice. A grievous sense of something gone wrong was settling into his gut. He fought the beery puke at the back of his throat. There were bottles of laxative on a shelf facing the girl, and Howard imagined his alimentary canal, of all things, mouth to anus, as a passage that epitomized civilization, and poked a finger into the wriggling girl's back to keep her facing the laxative. He massaged her collarbone. "No problem, gonna be all right."

Out front, Legat was still just on the other side of the curtain, rocking on the balls of his feet, eating more animal crackers. The crunch of the cookies filtered through the curtain.

"Hurry up!" Howard said. The girl jumped. "Mister?" she said, her voice rising on the last syllable.

"Yeah?"

"What are you going to do?"

"Don't worry, sweet cakes. No sweat." The small intestine gave the blood whatever was digestible. Howard massaged the girl's right collarbone without realizing what he was doing. He was filled with a vision of people as wormy creatures on sticks, padded with lots of flesh and cartilage, able to stand up and look around, but bio-logically not far removed from an earthworm, a long tube of mucus and tissue that survived by plundering whatever it could get into its gullet. It was a vision out of science fiction, some ghastly movie printed on his genes and developed without warning, the way light splashes into the eyes when bandages are removed after surgery.

The girl's bony shoulder blades arched out like undeveloped wings. "If you let me go, I'll just sit here. I won't call nobody."

Howard squeezed her neck gently. With his left hand, he lightly tapped her on the cheek. She quickly faced forward again. Howard looked around the storage room for some rope or twine. He had forgotten the extension cord in the car. He spotted a tube of crazyglue. Quickly he blindfolded the girl with a cleaning rag, making sure not to tie the knot too tight, and squiggled out two lines of crazyglue on either side of her. "Just open your hands and put them down next to you, sugar," he said. "One next to each leg, right there by your knees." Standing behind her, he grabbed hold of her wrists, as thin as tubes of toothpaste. "Right there. It won't hurt." He pressed her lifelines into the squiggles of crazyglue.

Legat pulled aside the curtain. "Somebody's coming," he said.

"Fuck," Howard said. "What's taking so long?"

Legat put on a white apron and stood behind the counter as though protecting the plate, his black plastic hood crumpled next to the register.

Howard thought about gagging the girl. He could see she un-derstood how tightly her hands were sealed to the box of reconsti-tuted lemon juice. But she would suffer no permanent damage, and Howard told himself that mattered in the scheme of things. He reached down and picked up an animal cracker from the floor and held it to her nostrils and then stuffed it into her mouth. "It's an owl," he said, though it wasn't.

"Thank you," she said. Howard listened as she chewed the cracker.

The bell to the store rang when the front door opened. "Gas?" somebody said.

"Broken," Legat answered. A man and a woman mumbled to

each other and then talked about highway mileage. Howard stared at them through the curtain. They loitered by a cooler of soda pop. The man prosecuted his case. "If we go four more hours, take turns, drink coffee, we can stop in Charlotte." The woman snorted. "No way. Charlotte's five or six hours at least from here. We're talking mountains. Even in daylight the drive's a blister." She had a clipped, silky way of making her point, a little like Hassie, so that the man seemed to deliberate more on how she sounded than on what she said. He was thinking motel room. He was thinking what they could do there. "Okay," he said, "we'll stay."

Howard nearly snickered. A worm on a crooked stick. If people are worms, then what's the difference? Whatever we do is what we do.

"Found what you wanted?" Legat said. "Sorry about the gas. Something's wrong with the pump."

"Those people never were here," Howard said to the girl. "You got that? They never came in. We came in, took the money and glued you down. And we didn't have any weapons. None. You got that? We had no weapons. We were not armed."

Legat, still deliberate, came into the back with a bottle of Windex. "Fingerprints," he said. "I did the register. You touch anything back here?" He eyed the girl. "What's your name, honey?"

"Roxanne?"

"Roxanne? You asking me or telling me? It don't matter, just listen up. You don't say anything about us. One guy came in here by himself. You got that?"

She nodded.

"I'm going to take your name from the Rolodex, Roxanne, and if we get any shit, any shit at all, I'll arrange a little accident. I have friends around here, they like to mess people up. You got that?"

"For chrissakes," Howard said, "don't scare her to death. Let's go."

"You done with that Windex?" Legat said.

Howard revved up the engine. Legat stood for a moment by the back door, then opened it, and went inside. He came out a minute later and gave Howard a thumbs-up sign. They squealed out of the lot. A few minutes later, they were cruising under one of

Knoxville's painted overpasses, the lines of I-40 sure and true. The last lights of the city faded in the rearview mirror and Howard listened to the sound of wind for miles, until the interstate veered southeast for the shrouded safety of the Great Smoky Mountains. Howard's adrenaline rush had chased most of the sugar from his blood and he had trouble staying awake. He needed some coffee or conversation, but Legat had nothing to say. Howard opened his window. The mountain air, at least, felt friendly, the way he had once felt at the ballpark. He had a rangy outfielder's disdain for detail and a power hitter's belief in the magic of concentration. Put him in the lineup and he might pole one into the street and save the game by reaching into the stands to complete a long out. But leave him on the bench and he connived.

He could remember nights when the stands had been filled to bursting with rowdy kids and their parents. The team would be giving away Frisbees or bats or some such thing. Once, a groaning teenage girl, covered with a thin blanket, had been carried out of the stadium on a stretcher. "We want to remind our young fans not to swing their new baseball bats in the vicinity of other paying customers," the ballpark announcer had said. "Put some pepper in that ball, boy!" a coach shouted from his position on the third-base line. "Go to page sixteen in your programs to see whether you have the winning number," the ballpark announcer blared over the p.a. system. "Your free small pizza may be waiting for you, piping hot." The dugout's corrugated tin awning clattered when a vendor rested his wire container of beer on it. Legat, who worked with the young pitchers, complaining mightily but teaching them the business, ground his jaw, pissed off at Kid Turkey, who had blinding speed but no control. Howard analyzed the hitch in Odell's swing; Odell was a clean-living hotshot kid who struck out every other time at bat but would take no advice from anyone. Howard saw himself in the boy but didn't want to coach when he could still play. Even from the bench, studying Odell, he could taste infield dirt on his lips and the bitterness of waiting to pinch-hit or substitute for some kid barely half his age.

In the Great Smokies, despite the danger of hairpin curves, he let his muscles do the driving. His mind, he told Hassie afterward, wandered from baseball to the owl. The large forward-set eyes of the owl followed him, as though the creature had adopted him. He couldn't let it go; at least it was better, and maybe even truer, than a worm on a crooked stick. "There's a river bridge I'm going to get to one day, once I do my time," he said. "It's cloud-covered like the Great Smokies, real dark in the distance, but still dim lit, like by lanterns. You know what I mean? I can hear the owl hooting on the other side of that bridge, hooting in the darkness."

Hassie stared at him. She didn't say a thing.

"What did you go back inside for?" Howard said to Legat, who was fully awake now, riding shotgun, elbow resting on the sill, fingers drumming on the plaid vinyl seat. They had reached the border between Tennessee and North Carolina and passed the tiny hamlet of Waterville.

"To kill her. No sense taking chances."

Afterward, after the verdict had been rendered and the courtroom cleared, after he had been taken to the prison where he would do his time, Howard dwelled on that moment. He nearly lost control of the car and, in prison, could still feel the way the car had ricocheted over the warning strips on the shoulder of the highway. He had slammed on his brakes and fishtailed before crunching to a stop. The engine had died. The driver of a rig behind them sat on his horn and the car shuddered in the truck's great gush of wind.

Legat tossed his empty carton of animal crackers out the window.

"Bullshit," Howard said.

"No, I killed her," Legat said evenly. "What else was I supposed to do? She saw my face. No man sees my face and lives. I did it the Brooklyn way. Took a piece of string." He demonstrated, miming strangulation. "I garroted her. Took a minute or so. She's out of her misery, poor thing."

"That's some story," Howard said, hands tight on the wheel. "I haven't heard it before. You read it in a magazine?" Little bumps appeared on the left side of his face, as though a case of poison oak was developing in the mountain air. Storm clouds rumbled over the Bald Mountains.

Legat's face was contorted, as though his neurons and synapses were misfiring. "What's wrong?" He stuck out his lower lip, as though pouting. "Did I do something wrong?"

"If that girl is strangled, you're fishmeat."

"Let me tell you something. You've been fucking with my head for weeks. You're the one who's the oldest goddamn player in the league. You had your chance and blew it." He pumped a catcher's crooked, arthritic finger in Howard's face. "The only reason I pulled this job tonight was because you had me thinking I was finished, too."

Howard kept his hands on the wheel and stared past Legat toward the faraway cloud-covered summit of Mt. Sterling. "You saw my maps. You know what we were supposed to do, and what we weren't supposed to do." Even the jangling of adrenaline in his veins barely kept him coherent. "Just for the sake of argument. What would we gain if you really killed the girl?"

"She's a witness, you asshole."

"Witness to what? Petty theft? Unless you really did something to her, we might not even make the papers." He reconsidered and shrugged. "First offense? What we gonna get? A year, maybe two? That's it."

Legat turned away from Howard, who pulled back onto the highway, his entire face by now on fire with some kind of rash. Legat counted the money. "Maybe a couple hundred here, maybe less. Shit." He scratched at his face. "Those goddamn bags. They give me an itch. What they made out of?"

"Petroleum. Louisiana oil." His sinuses were clogged, ears popping.

"Shit," Legat said. "This is chump change. Are we morons, or what?"

"Why *did* you go back in there?" Howard said. "I want to hear you say it, Legat. Say you didn't hurt the girl."

Legat was still fishing out bills from his pockets. "I wanted to check her out. I was the one who took the bag off my head. You re-member that? Suppose she talks? You say we should let her live. I say we kill her. We disagree. That's all. Let's agree to disagree."

"Bullshit," Howard said.

Legat relented. "Look, she's a kid. I wanted to tell her a little more about my friends in town, what kind of animals they are. I fed her a candy bar, one of those Snickers. I like the name Roxanne. When I caught little league in Brooklyn, my girlfriend's name was Roxanne. I think I'm a little in love."

Howard let out a deep breath.

"What a night." He stared into gashes of lightning on the hori-zon. "That was the stupidest thing I've ever done. It's like there's something inside of me I need to break open, and the only way to do it is to do something crazy." Just keep the car pointed ahead, he told himself, take the turns in stride, up hill and down dale, whip through Asheville without a passing glance, hump by the Black Mountain exit, then coast for miles to the piedmont, car in neutral, heartbreak turns whizzing by, truckers riding their brakes and praying they wouldn't need the gravel runoff chutes. It would take guts to turn your truck off the highway and hope for mercy and luck instead of the abyss.

Afterward, he told and retold the story and Hassie listened until there was nothing else to tell. There was no other story to tell. She was no longer his wife. Everything concerning the two of them was over with, except for Sally and the words between them. She was the woman who listened so he could serve his time. That was how he thought of it. It was a kindness. She was more than a worm on a stick. She was a better friend to him than he had been to her, but it was too late to do anything about it. "What are you going to tell Sally?"

Hassie winced. It was their last visit. She was dressed in a blue print blouse, a wide belt, and jeans. Howard guessed her new boyfriend had given her an ultimatum. "I don't know," she said. "I won't know until I sit with her and talk. When you sit down to talk, things have a way of getting said. You know what I mean."

"Yeah," he said. "Yeah, baby, I know."

After she left, he knew that his only hope of finding his destiny was to live alone in his cell with the owl, its black eyes gone gray and its painted wings as fluffy as fur in a dream. He no longer knew if the owl that he had given to his daughter would protect her or not. Either way, he came to believe, serving out his time, that he was traveling with the owl, ever further and faster, on a planet that carried him forever away from his origins and from the people he loved.

ROUGH GOD GOES RIDING

I moved to St. Cloud to get an education and stayed, working as a housepainter, until duty called. My great-grandfather had served in the Great War, my grandfather had served in the Good War, and my father had gone to another one. It was my turn. They sent me straight to a theater of operation, a place where my ancestors once lived. It had a name nobody in my company, even the lieutenant, knew how to pronounce.

Our barracks had concertina wire and guard towers. It was like we were prisoners and not liberators. The sergeant said, cocking his hat like a gun and placing his hand on a shoulder of Carol, "These people need our help, because we're Americans and they're not." He dismissed us, then called us back to pass out leaflets that promised a free Florida vacation to anyone who volunteered for another year of overseas duty.

From the tiny slit next to my bunk I could see the church spire in the village, could see cupolas and bell towers. Sometimes I glimpsed skiffs slicing through the faraway blue water. The shelling had stopped when we arrived because we'd let everyone know we'd kick butt if it didn't. I would stare from the slit through its shatter-proof mesh and wonder what the place was like. If I strained my eyes, I could see what looked like an amusement park with roller-coaster tracks snaking through the hills and bright lights sparkling after dark. "That's the fleshpot of the peninsula," the lieutenant said. "That's where the Queen of England lives." He showed me a photograph.

It was months before I saw the place for myself. Behind the concertina wire, we were protected from the villagers. They no longer bombed one another, but half the countryside was booby-trapped and unspent shells littered the land. We were kept busy with calisthenics and maneuvers, with language lessons and weapons training. I had a facility for language acquisition that surprised me; my Fosdek became not fluent but serviceable. Maybe it was racial memory. "Anyway," the lieutenant told me, "everybody knows *some* English." Most nights, it was lights-out and straight off to bed, all of us too exhausted for anything else. We got the occasional beer, the occasional beefsteak barbecue. Once, a band was brought in with trumpets, saxophones, and cornets, with tubas and a bass drum. But social intercourse was strictly controlled. As for the constant stream of refugees who stumbled past the gatehouse on the road near the mess hall, they looked like barbarians to me, all right.

I wasn't meant to be a soldier. I didn't like dismantling, oiling, and reassembling the light machine gun for target practice. We sprayed better than six hundred rounds a minute into straw-filled dummies meant to resemble various factions from the local population. "Shoot the fuckers," the sergeant told us. "You're Americans, and they're not."

I took a liking to Carol. There was a high infectious laugh and a whimsical way of biting on one nail when she looked at me. We would eat our beefsteaks and talk. We were both from the Midwest, and felt a little funny around people from other places. We never put it quite that way, of course, but I took Carol for a kindred spirit, an innocent like me, until I noticed the way her eyes tightened around the sniper scope. She would blast target after target with cheerleader relish, and lick her lips with satisfaction. She was so good they made her Delta Force; she scored one hundred percent hits at six hundred and fifty yards and better than ninety percent at eleven hundred yards.

I did all right myself and one day the lieutenant pulled me aside and set up special lessons for me on the shooting range with a 9 mm semiautomatic. "I've got my eye on you," he said. "You know how to be secret. You're picking up the lingo faster than anyone else is. You're agent material." I learned how to mix ordinary household chemicals to make bombs that could level a city block. "This is like candle and blood, dude," the sergeant told me one night. "You're becoming one of the elect. Did you re-up for that Florida vacation yet?" They taught me how to be a killer, worked me to the limits of my endurance. "You'll be grateful out in the world." They let me grow back my hair, intensified my language-immersion program. I wasn't supposed to talk in anything but Fosdek so that I would feel more comfortable outside the wire.

I wrote letters home and mailed them every day. But the letters were never answered. All any of us received were advertising brochures, contest announcements, political newsletters from local representatives, invitations to join record clubs or to buy special-edition ceramicware embossed with patriotic imagery.

The local castle was close to the village. One cold day the captain took the company there for some R and R. I needed it. I was waking up every night screaming. Besides, there was a man in my platoon, T-Bo Malloy, a weightlifter with a body like concrete, who caught me talking to Carol. He let me know she was off-limits unless he gave the word. "I'm kind of like, you know, her bodyguard?" he said. "Don't take it personal, but you're becoming the sort of person she's not allowed to associate with."

At the castle, set on a slope and tilted at an almost impossible angle, the captain paid our zlotnys for us and ordered us to stay in a group, but Carol and I managed to get lost while the others walked the parapets, sighted from the battlements, took snapshots of the turrets, the drawbridge, and the dungeon. Carol and I ended up holding hands and fooling around in the dim light of a winding stairwell which led to the chapel. Touching the thick, wily hair on one of her arms sent the blood. "I can't kill anybody," I confessed to her. "I'm not made that way. I belong back in St. Cloud."

She told me I looked a little like the boyfriend she had back home. "Only he's not my boyfriend anymore," she said.

On the bus back to the barracks, an army surplus job that

rocked on rough road, T-Bo was beside himself, flexing his gigantic biceps. He sat next to me, his immensity forcing me against the window. I tried to ignore him, stared at the villages, now overhung by dark clouds. The cold, northeasterly bora wind rapped against the glass. Gaunt-faced starving children in rags waved at me. I wondered what their parents could be thinking, wrapping them in nothing when the wind was so cold. I wanted to throw them a candy bar or something, but the window was screwed shut.

T-Bo squeezed my wrist. "You son of a bitch," he said. "You know I could break every bone in your body and the lieutenant would look the other way. You know that, don't you? Don't contaminate that girl."

"Contaminate?" I said, loud enough to attract attention.

"That's two strikes," he whispered. "One more, you're done."

Back at the barracks, the pace of training accelerated and before I knew it spring had arrived. It was like there was a glass curtain between me and the rest of the company. And T-Bo was always in the picture, between the regular troops and me. "I've fixed it for you," he said to me once. "I've arranged things. Trust me." By then, the bora wind was a distant memory. The lieutenant made me an official infiltrator, provided me with papers, put me in civvies, gave me some currency, dollars, zlotnys—I could never keep them straight—and sent me to live in the village.

My fear of getting found out or shot followed me everywhere; I carried my 9 mm strapped to an ankle under a cuff of my workpants. I didn't think I could shoot anyone, even with my training, because I was a nice guy, American through and through. But the villagers were nothing like the fun-loving folk I had imagined from my narrow bunk. Some of them were miners with smudged faces who probably never saw daylight and who stayed as drunk as they could manage. Some were in the trades, counted every zlotny, and kept their eyes on me until I was out of sight. I got along best with the farmers who came into town twice a week to get drunk. My father is a farmer, and they're all alike, talking weather and maintaining a barren kind of dignity. I also got along with the laborers who made their money climbing up and down the mountains, working as mules for employers they refused to name. In the taverns, they would listen ferociously to pop muzica.

By bribing a tradesman, I got a job in a sort of kiosk near the harbor, on a shell-pocked road that also happened to be the road from the barracks. Soldiers passed all the time. Carol stopped once to buy a snack, but there was no giveaway recognition in her eyes or in mine. Refugees, carrying everything they owned on their backs, stopped and begged for crumbs. I resented them for not dying.

I lived there almost a year. I even had a woman for a while, one who had lost fingers on her hands. Then she disappeared and I forgot about her. I was paying my own way. I had a room over a barbershop. Of course, I also had the barbershop wired and reported on a regular basis to the lieutenant. I began to feel guilty about my double life; I found myself identifying with the rough pleasures and bitter views of the villagers. It was great to smoke a cigarette with them in a coffeehouse now and then without feeling like a criminal, the way I did back in St. Cloud, where so many people believe that destiny is a thing we can control, that life is like clay that can be molded, that the right vitamins can make you never get sick.

In the village, we drank sodny by the gallon, hated almost everyone, and didn't disguise it. Why should we? It felt great to say, "I hate those bastards," something I had never said before in my life. "Stinking Americans," I'd mutter under my breath. I saw what life was. I'd listen maliciously to local tales of gunrunning refugees raped and stoned to death, of villagers with the wrong blood in their veins who had to be beaten until they left town once and for all. It was like the Old West. "They're in the forbidden village now, the one down the highway," I was told. "Where the Queen of England lives. If you ever go there, take some dynamite with you. Blow some of those fucking cunts to kingdom come."

One dark night, so drunk I could barely follow my own thoughts, I stumbled into the street and saw Carol with several of her friends. It was a cloudy night without a moon and I followed at a distance, lonely, making up my mind to approach her. Then I saw her kissing some guy who looked like T-Bo. My thought was this: what would it be like to kill him and rape her? My fellow villagers had told me rape was the best sex you could get. Could I justify raping Carol in the name of national security? Wasn't she a refugee, after all, someone here in my village without permission, spying on us, usurping my job? But somehow I lost her on the streets built atop one another like a winding staircase. I wanted to fall down in the dark and weep. What had they done to me? Where did I belong? I didn't know who I was anymore. Besides, what if we did stop the killing? Wouldn't it just be a matter of time until the villagers received coupons for free Florida vacations? There was something about tribal genocide I had come to admire. At least they cared enough about something to kill each other over it.

Dogs were howling all around me. I kept walking in the dark, aiming for some faraway lights, until I was surrounded by strange structures and realized where I was. It was the forbidden village. Muzica was everywhere, violins in the restaurants, brass bands clanging away under streetlights. Ladies of the evening surrounded me, but they weren't crudely dressed. They wore gray, tailored suits and carried attaché cases. Banners fluttered from the tilted, half-timbered eaves, and a woman with wingtip shoes put an arm around my waist. "You ready for a date, honey?" she said. "No, no, just looking," I said, whereupon a man in a bright gypsy vest stepped in front of me, his hands balled into fists. "Something wrong with her, brother?" he said. "I'm just not in the mood," I answered. He gripped my wrist. I thought he might break a bone. After that, everything blurs together, but I know that I knew my cover was blown. Still reeling from drink, I made my way from alley to alley, avoiding scattered debris from the war. I went from rooftop to rooftop, keeping to the shadows, putting into practice everything I had learned. Escape was the only motive. I came upon a kind of roller coaster that transported miners to and from the mountains. With the sound of dogs and whistles behind me, I began to climb up the narrow-gauge track straight into the sky until I was high enough to look down at the colored banners and strolling figures of the village that from above promised so much pleasure. The darkness around the village was dotted with the flickering lights of refugee campfires and the occasional flash of munitions. Shots rang out below and the heel of one foot started to sting terribly when a bullet found its mark. The tracks swayed in the wind. It struck me that I was climbing a ladder into the clouds. Attacked by vertigo, I closed my eyes, frozen with fear, until I heard the rumble of guide wheels on the tracks and then saw the roller coaster approaching from below, crawling up the incline. I swung myself over the edge of the tracks and hung from the scaffold. When the open cars were passing above me, I pulled myself up and jumped aboard. Minutes later I flung myself into a farmer's field and went limping along until a convertible approached. I stuck out my thumb and the vehicle stopped. The two women in it had long hair. One of them was the Queen of England. The other was Carol. "Hop in, lover boy," the Queen of England said. Carol looked at me funny, biting a nail. I crunched in between them and we drove along fast, our hair whipping in the wind. Carol loosened up and held my hand. We smoked cigarettes and drank vodka, threw the butts and empty bottles at the refugees who clogged the road. "This is what it's like to be an American!" I screamed. But then the Queen of England pulled a gun on me. "Get out!" she said. "I'm right behind you." She had a Galil Sniping Rifle, the buttstock still folded. She disappeared off into the weeds. A Galil could score a head shot at three hundred meters. The lieutenant clapped me on the back. "Mission accomplished!" he screamed. "We contained the crisis. I can't tell you everything, but you'll definitely get a medal. You ready for that Florida vacation?" I didn't know what to say. Stalling for time, I took out a pocketknife and went to work on the bullet in the heel of my foot. I cut away the sock. Once the wound was bandaged, they gave me a pill and took me back to the barracks.

But something inside me was finished forever.

I never took them up on the vacation in Miami. Now I'm back in St. Cloud, housepainting again, being an American. I did my duty.

Hey, did you do yours?

ACKNOWLEDGMENTS

Most of these stories were first published in different form in the following journals: *ACM*, *Ascent*, the *Chattahoochee Review*, the *Cream City Review*, the *Great River Review*, *Image*, *North Dakota Quarterly*, the *Quarterly*, *San Jose Studies* and *South Dakota Review*. My thanks to the editors of these publications.

"The Battle of New Orleans," which appeared in the *North Dakota Quarterly*, was performed in four sections on November 3, 1995, as part of *The Wrecking Ball*, a multimedia event directed by Richard Morgan and produced by the Theater of the Invisible Guests.

"Suddenly I Meet Your Face," which appeared in *ACM* as "Blood Cells," was performed in 1992 as a rock opera adapted and directed by Todd Deming.

I also wish to thank the Loft and the McKnight Foundation for a Loft-McKnight Award of Distinction in Creative Prose, the C.I.E.S. and the Fulbright organization for two Fulbright Awards, Ragdale for a residency, the Minnesota State Arts Board for a Fellowship, and Minnesota State University at Moorhead for a Creative Activity Grant. Some of these stories were written with the help of these various grants and awards.

Finally, I want to thank my friends who read earlier drafts of these stories—their interest means a great deal to me—and everyone at New Rivers Press for their tact and hard labor.

Alan Davis is the author of *Rumors from the Lost World* and for a dozen years has coedited *American Fiction*, an annual anthology chosen by *Writer's Digest* as one of the top fifteen short story publications in the country. His work appears in notable literary journals and newspapers and has received numerous awards. He grew up in Louisiana, has lived in Slovenia and Indonesia, among other places, and now teaches in the English and M.F.A. programs at Minnesota State University at Moorhead, which is located just across the Red River from Fargo, North Dakota.